CITIZEN K-9

ALSO BY DAVID ROSENFELT

ANDY CARPENTER NOVELS

Best in Snow

Dog Eat Dog

Silent Bite

Muzzled

Dachshund Through the Snow

Bark of Night

Deck the Hounds

Rescued

Collared

The Twelve Dogs of Christmas

Outfoxed

Who Let the Dog Out?

Hounded

Unleashed

Leader of the Pack

One Dog Night

Dog Tags

New Tricks

Play Dead

Dead Center

Sudden Death

Bury the Lead

First Degree

Open and Shut

K TEAM NOVELS

Animal Instinct

The K Team

THRILLERS

Black and Blue

Fade to Black

Blackout

Without Warning

Airtight

Heart of a Killer

On Borrowed Time

Down to the Wire

Don't Tell a Soul

NONFICTION

Lessons from Tara: Life Advice from the World's Most Brilliant
Dog

Dogtripping: 25 Rescues, 11 Volunteers, and 3 RVs on Our Canine
Cross-Country Adventure

CITIZEN K-9

DAVID ROSENFELT

MINOTAUR
BOOKS
NEW YORK

First published in the United States by Minotaur Books, an imprint of St. Martin's Publishing Group

www.minotaurbooks.com

Designed by Omar Chapa

Library of Congress Cataloging-in-Publication Data

Names: Rosenfelt, David, author.
Title: Citizen K-9 / David Rosenfelt.
Description: First edition. | New York : Minotaur Books, 2022. | Series: K team novels
Identifiers: LCCN 2021047574 | ISBN 9781250828934 (hardcover) | ISBN 9781250828941 (ebook)
Subjects: LCGFT: Novels.
Classification: LCC PS3618.O838 C58 2022 | DDC 813/.6—dc23
LC record available at https://lccn.loc.gov/2021047574

Our books may be purchased in bulk for promotional, educational, or business use. Please contact your local bookseller or the Macmillan Corporate and Premium Sales Department at 1-800-221-7945, extension 5442, or by email at MacmillanSpecialMarkets@macmillan.com.

First Edition: 2022

10 9 8 7 6 5 4 3 2 1

CITIZEN K-9

LIFE HAD TAKEN A DECIDEDLY POSITIVE TURN FOR CHRIS VOGEL.

He wasn't free from problems, and he was all too conscious that his were for the most part self-inflicted. But he had two sources of money to help him out of trouble, and now he had a way to ensure that he was safe from legal jeopardy. Almost a literal "get out of jail free" card.

Vogel also had something else going for him, something he never expected and had never before experienced. That was an excitement, an invigoration, that came from turning his life over to fate. At first he thought the feeling was nonsense, a ridiculous but violent diversion from the mess that was his life, and he silently mocked it. But after time he indulged it and lived it, and the truth was he gradually became addicted to it.

After all, the sensation was intoxicating and offered a feeling of freedom unlike any other he had ever imagined. And he was clear minded enough to know that, as counterintuitive as it sounded, the freedom actually came from giving up his freedom.

Never had the feeling been stronger than it was at that moment. It was a more powerful high than he had ever experienced with drugs, and he had certainly done his share in that area. But on this night it was accompanied by almost paralyzing nervousness; he had never done anything like this and never thought that he would.

The high, and the nervousness, left no room for guilt. Maybe that would come later, maybe not. It hadn't so far, at least not enough to cause him to stop. If it grew and became a significant factor, he would deal with it and move on.

The evening had been a strange one for Vogel, mainly because he had never pictured himself attending a high school reunion. The event itself was boring, as he knew it would be. With the exception of a select few, he had not seen these people in years and didn't care if he ever saw them again. He'd had no use for them back in the day; nothing had changed in that regard, especially since the disdain had always been mutual.

The truth is that he would never have attended the event if this plan had not been in place. The last thing he wanted to do was revisit any part of high school. But Vogel wasn't bored; he was anxious. He knew where the night was going to end up, and he could think of nothing else.

Getting Kim Baskin to leave with him, as planned, had proven to be easy. She bought his story fully and completely, and they had left together in his car. She believed him when he promised they would be back soon.

They had driven less than three miles when he pulled into a rest area off the Garden State Parkway. "What are we doing here?" she asked, slight worry creeping into her voice.

He smacked the steering wheel in feigned frustration. "Damn. The car is starting to overheat. I've got to get some water. This happened the other day also, but my mechanic said he fixed it. I'll just be a minute."

He pulled up to the small building, but didn't turn off the car. Instead he opened the passenger door window from his driver's side controls.

"Get out of the car."

It wasn't Vogel's voice; another man had come to the window with a gun. Baskin let out a small scream of terror and looked toward Vogel, but all he said was "You heard him. Get out."

The man at the passenger side pulled the door open, grabbed Baskin, and pulled her out. She tried to scream but it caught in her throat. "You too," the man said, pointing the gun at Vogel. "Get out."

"What are you talking about, Z? You know what we're supposed to do."

"I know exactly what I am supposed to do. I said get out of the car."

Vogel was confused and scared, but he did as he was told. The man called Z handcuffed them to each other and then to a pole inside his van. He placed tight gags over their mouths so they could not communicate or yell for help; it was all they could do to breathe. Then he took the clear plastic bag out of his pocket and left it in the glove compartment of Vogel's car. Once he had done that, he removed any trace of his fingerprints inside the car and closed the door. He went back to the van and drove off with his captives.

Vogel, handcuffed in the back, had long ago begun to share Baskin's panic; this was not what was supposed to happen. All he could think of was that maybe Espinosa had learned what he had done and had somehow gotten to Z. But how could that be?

Vogel would never learn whether he was correct, and he and Baskin would never be seen again.

I'M A COP.

Not technically; I don't get paid by the Paterson Police Department anymore, and I no longer have a badge and a uniform. I don't drive a police car, and I can't arrest people, which was a fun part of the job. I still carry a gun, but it's one that I own personally.

The bottom line is that if you asked the Paterson chief of police if Corey Douglas was on the force, he would say, "Who's Corey Douglas?" And then after he looked me up, he'd say, "Oh, he was a sergeant in the K-9 unit. But not anymore; he put in his time and retired."

But I have learned since retiring a couple of years ago that the feeling of being a police officer never goes away. We become retired cops, not ex-cops. Especially in cases like mine, since as a private investigator I have sort of stayed in the action.

The "cop feeling" is most pronounced at times like this, when I visit the old precinct. Everything just falls into place the moment I walk in the door. I can remember the old rhythms, the rituals I used to have; it all feels so damn normal. I feel like I should be going to my locker to get ready to go out in the field.

I don't come here often; I don't want to seem like a hanger-on. And I certainly don't regret putting in for retirement; the grind was getting to me and it was absolutely the right time to go.

But occasionally I'll go out with a couple of buddies from the old days, and sometimes I'll meet them here. And a few times I've brought Simon Garfunkel with me, because they all love and miss him. Simon is a German shepherd who was my partner on the force for seven years and who is now a valued member of our investigative group, which we call the K Team.

The other members of the team, except for Simon, are here with me today at the precinct. They are Laurie Collins, also an ex-cop from the Paterson PD, and Marcus Clark. I'm not just saying this, but we are kick-ass investigators, and we make a damn good team.

We're not paying a social call today; we've been summoned to a meeting with Pete Stanton, captain in charge of the Homicide Division of the Paterson PD. None of us has any idea why he wants to see us. I doubt it's to arrest us, since it's been a while since we've killed anyone, other than in self-defense.

I know Pete, though not well. Our lives never really intersected when I was on the force. Laurie knows him a lot better, mainly because Pete is a sports bar buddy of Laurie's husband, attorney Andy Carpenter.

Andy is not a part of the K Team, though when he takes a case, he usually employs us as his investigators. Andy and Laurie are wealthy due to Andy's inheritance and some lucrative cases. The money has not done much for Andy's work ethic. He's a great lawyer who would just as soon stop lawyering and work instead in service of his passion, which is dog rescue.

Pete and Andy, along with their other friend Vince Sanders, basically limit their conversations to throwing insults at each other. They never get offended; I think it's more of a competition. They're like high school kids without the potential for future growth and maturity.

I'm the last one to arrive, and when I do, we're brought in to meet with Pete. On the way, Laurie and I see a bunch of our old friends, who greet us, but we don't stop to chat. I'm sure they're wondering what the hell we're doing here, and we're unable to enlighten them.

Pete greets us with a smile, a handshake for Marcus and me, and a hug for Laurie. Pete offers us something to drink, and Laurie and I ask for water, which he takes from a small refrigerator in the corner of the office. Marcus declines with a shake of the head. Marcus doesn't say much, and when he does, it is pretty much unintelligible to everyone but Laurie.

"Andy specifically asked me not to send you his best, and he wanted me to inform you of that fact," Laurie says. "I regret to say that I am married to a four-year-old."

Pete frowns. "Yeah, I saw him at Charlie's last night. I actually don't think he has a 'best,' but he has plenty of 'worst.' And you can tell him I said that. He defending any slimeballs this week?"

"No, he's still into client avoidance."

It's because of Andy's attitude toward work that we're forced to take on other clients to fill the gap.

"So why did you call this meeting, Pete?" It's my style; whenever there is a chase, I tend to cut to it.

"We've had some budget cuts."

"We're not part of your budget, Pete, so I'm afraid you can't cut us," Laurie says. "You looking for a loan?"

"I'll take whatever you can spare. But if you think things were tight when you were on the force, that's nothing like it is now. Our new mayor thinks he can solve the city's problems by cutting back on our funding. And it's not just us; he's even doing it to the fire department. Good luck with that; the mayor better not smoke in bed."

"And we come in where in this story, exactly?" Laurie asks.

"I'm sure you know this, since it was the same when you were here, but we have different budget pots. Most of them are empty, but the consultant pot is pretty full. That's because we haven't been hiring any. That's about to change. It's nuts that we can't pay for more cops, we can't even authorize overtime, but we can pay for consultants. Pisses me off, actually, but it is what it is."

"So you want to hire us as consultants?" I ask. "Is that what we're doing now? Consulting?"

"Not really; I want to hire you as investigators. Your fee would still come out of the consultant pot."

"What is it we'd be investigating?"

"In a way that's up to you. I've been trying for a long time to form a unit within the department to focus on cold homicide cases. That's never going to happen internally, at least not in my lifetime. We barely have the manpower for current cases, and people keep getting themselves killed. So you are my chance to tackle the cold cases out of this other pot."

"How would it work?" Laurie asks.

"I figured I'd show you three or four cases that interest me, and you pick one of them to focus on at a time. You'll have pretty much free rein, and the support of the department. I would just want you to keep me updated on what you're doing, so I don't get any surprises if you ruffle any feathers. You guys do have a tendency to ruffle feathers."

Laurie turns to Marcus. "Marcus?"

Marcus nods slightly, which for him represents a major endorsement and an enthusiastic yes.

"Corey?"

I nod as well. "Works for me. You know our rate? Feather ruffling does not come cheap."

Pete shrugs. "I have no idea what your rate is, but I'm sure you're overpaid. You should deal with accounting on that, but I can tell you that it won't be a problem. It's a pretty big pot. So we're agreed on this?"

"We are," Laurie says. "When do we start?"

"Here's a rundown of four cases . . . just a paragraph or two on each. You might be familiar with some of them. Let me know what interests you. If none of these appeal to you, there are others to pick from. We have no shortage of unsolved crimes, as Andy has pointed out to me on many occasions."

Pete hands two sheets of paper to each of us, and we glance at them quickly. I am familiar with two of the three on the first page. Laurie and I turn to the second page at the same time, and after a few seconds we both look up and make eye contact.

Nothing needs to be said between us.

"Pete," I say, "this is a no-brainer."

I DON'T REMEMBER MUCH ABOUT THE NIGHT ITSELF.

It was seven years ago, which unfortunately these days seems to be the outside edge of my memory statute of limitations. But it also wasn't particularly eventful.

It was the fifteen-year reunion for my Paterson Eastside High School graduating class. Eastside is sort of famous, having been the setting for *Lean on Me,* starring Morgan Freeman. He played Joe Clark, a principal with some rather controversial methods for running a school. The movie was shot on location at Eastside, but that was well before my time.

Looking back, I think that fifteen years might be too soon to have a reunion. It's nice to see everyone, or almost everyone, but it isn't enough time to let people brag and lie about what they've accomplished in life. Maybe that's the reason that the evening seemed curiously lacking in emotion; I think nostalgia takes more time to incubate and fully form.

Laurie was there too; I only found that out recently when she told me. I didn't know her back then, so would have had no reason to remember her presence. It wasn't her class; she was a year behind me. She knew so many people in my class that she and some of her friends decided to crash our reunion. I can't imagine that anyone complained; Laurie's the room-brightening type.

Even though I now think of the night as significant because of what ultimately transpired, it was a fairly bland but inoffensive evening. The event took place at the Woodcliff Lake Hilton, a nice enough venue, and as I recall, they had a pretty decent DJ playing the music of our high school years.

There were plenty of balloons in an obvious effort to make it seem festive, with limited success. I think that when places like that use balloons, then by definition they're trying too hard.

I didn't bring a date; I was going out with Laura Blanchard at the time, but she wasn't from Paterson and wasn't interested in coming. Or I wasn't interested in bringing her . . . I can't remember which. I'm sure I wouldn't have wanted her to find out that I had been lying about my success playing for Eastside's sports teams.

Chris Vogel was there that night, as was Kim Baskin. It's said that they didn't arrive together, and I didn't notice if they spent much time with each other at the event. Kim was sort of a friend of mine; we had dated once in high school and remained friendly after that. Not close friends, but we liked each other. She was a nice if not terribly memorable person, although people certainly remember her now.

I didn't know Chris at all. Laurie says she knew him but not well; he was not a member of the group she hung out with in high school. He wasn't what one would call socially successful, but he was certainly a good student. He went on to school at Dartmouth, which was not exactly on my list of schools to apply to. In fact, there were no schools on that list; I went to the police academy and never looked back.

I left the event fairly early, or at least that's how I remember it. I went with a bunch of other guys to the Bonfire, a Paterson restaurant that was sort of our hangout in high school. I don't know if Chris and Kim were still at the hotel when I left; I just didn't notice either way. I would have had no reason to.

Witnesses said that they left together, and as far as I know, those same witnesses were the last people to see either of them alive . . . or dead.

Chris Vogel and Kim Baskin simply disappeared. Vogel's car was found abandoned at a rest stop on the Garden State Parkway, not more than five minutes from the hotel. Baskin's remained in the parking lot at the hotel. No clues indicated what happened to them; they just vanished from the face of the earth.

It became a huge story at the time, and occasionally over the years people reported sighting one or the other. They've been spotted more times than Amelia Earhart. But each time it has turned out to be false.

They have not been seen since, and they are now legally presumed dead. No one knows how they died, where they died, or, most important, why they died. For that matter, no one can know with total certainty *if* they died.

Now the K Team will try to change all that.

"I DIDN'T EVEN KNOW ABOUT IT FOR A FEW DAYS AFTER THAT NIGHT," I SAY.

I'm out to dinner with Dani Kendall at the Avenue Bistro in Verona. We come here almost every night for a couple of reasons. First of all, they have an outdoor section where we can sit and bring Simon Garfunkel; they even provide a water bowl and a biscuit. The biscuit is dessert; we usually order mixed vegetables for Simon.

The other reason, which is why we always go out, is that Dani and I vie for the honor of being designated the worst cook in America. I'm probably slightly better at it than she is; for instance, I can successfully make toast. Dani openly and unashamedly admits her incompetence in the kitchen, and though that is refreshing, it's not all that filling.

Dani and I recently entered the fifth stage of our relationship. In order, the stages have been:

Dating, and me trying to find enough fault with her to break up. That's my normal style, though in this case it didn't come close to working, which is why I moved on to stage two.

Me realizing that stage one wasn't working, and that the faults just weren't there. Since everyone has faults, I figured she must be deceiving me, which made me consider ending it just on principle. Who wants a relationship based on deception? But I couldn't seem to pull the trigger, so it was on to phase three.

Dating steadily and exclusively, with me switching to worrying that she would find fault with me and end it. So I deceived her, to cover up my faults. I've always felt that there needs to be some deception in every relationship to keep it healthy. I succeeded in fooling her, which brought us to stage four.

Dani staying over at my house maybe half the nights, though keeping her own apartment. That way we were able to make a commitment to each other, without really committing. If it sounds unsatisfying, that's because it was. Hence . . . stage five.

Dani keeping her apartment, but basically moving in full-time with me. That's where we are now, and it's going just fine, thank you.

I think we both realize that additional stages are in our future, but we're not going there yet. She seems as leery of marriage as I am, though I'm losing track of why I have that attitude. In my case it's a knee-jerk reaction, emphasis on *jerk*.

"It wasn't big news right away?" Dani asks. "Two people go missing without a trace? I would think that would be the lead story on any given night."

I nod. "It was, eventually. But at first there was no clear evidence of foul play, and no real reason to suspect any. The police thought it was more logical that they ran off together and would eventually show up. They were unmarried adults; for all anyone knew they were drinking piña coladas in Barbados for a week. I actually heard about it before the public because it was talked about at the precinct when it became apparent that something was wrong."

"Were either of them in a relationship with someone else at the time?"

"I don't think Vogel was, but I'm pretty sure that Kim was engaged. To my knowledge her fiancé was never considered a suspect, even though I'm sure they must have looked at him."

"So the department will be sending you all the information? What they uncovered and what they didn't?"

"Yes. Once people started getting concerned, the investigation got pretty intense. At least I assume so; I wasn't a part of it."

"Maybe they just ran off and started a new life."

"Maybe, but that's not that easy to do. And it would mean cutting themselves off from everyone . . . family, friends, career. And you just take off after a reunion? Doesn't seem likely, but we'll know more when we get into it."

Dani looks at me and smiles. "You love this, don't you?"

Even though she ended the sentence with "don't you?," it wasn't really a question. She knows me pretty well.

"I do. It's a puzzle, and I like to figure it out. I enjoy the process."

Another smile from Dani. "And if there are bad guys involved who think they've gotten away with something for all these years, you want to show them otherwise. It's what drives you."

"Guilty as charged."

"You're a cop."

I can't deny it. "I'm a cop."

OUR INITIAL MEETING TO GO OVER THE CASE IS AT LAURIE'S.

That's pretty much the norm for us because Simon likes to play with Tara, Andy and Laurie's golden retriever. They have two other dogs as well. Hunter is a pug who is eager but can't quite handle the wrestling action between Simon and Tara. He tries but gets pushed aside.

Sebastian, their basset hound, would rather sleep than play. He'd rather sleep than anything, except maybe eat. I can see myself being like Sebastian when and if I grow up.

Pete has had three sets of all the documentation relevant to the investigation sent to the house, at Laurie's request. He's also sent it electronically, but we are old-fashioned and like to feel the paper in our hands. So the first thing we need to do, before we can discuss it and strategize, is go through it.

That's not quite right. The first thing to do is get lunch. To that end, Laurie calls in Andy, who has been watching television in the den. "Andy, we're hungry."

"I'll alert the media."

"Any chance if I order from the deli, you'd pick it up for us?"

"Very slim; I just don't see it happening."

"Thank you, my supportive husband."

This back-and-forth is typical of their relationship. Andy pretends to protest and assert himself, but ultimately allows Laurie to call the shots. Behind all of it is an obvious, mutual respect.

Marcus and I give Laurie our orders, and after Andy does as well, she calls it in. Before Andy leaves to get it, he asks, "Should I put this on the K Team tab?"

"We don't have a tab," Laurie says.

"I'll start keeping one."

We start going through the documents, and after lunch we continue for a short while. My approach in these situations, which is apparently shared by Laurie and Marcus, is to skim through documents, just to get a sense of what is there. There will be time to intensely study them later, but for now we just have to understand what we're dealing with.

One thing is immediately obvious: the solution is not to be found in here. The investigating officers, who I know from my time on the force, never got a good handle on the case. It started out a mystery and remained one. They did a lot of legwork, but accomplished little, if anything.

When we take a case, one person usually takes the lead. Marcus doesn't like to be in that role; his preference is to take an assignment and follow through on it. Often that can involve danger; no one on the planet is tougher, more frightening, or more fearless than Marcus. I don't just mean this planet; I mean any planet.

I'm able to handle myself pretty well for the physical stuff, and Marcus makes me look like a wilting flower.

Laurie suggests that I take the lead, and I'm fine with that. We'll divvy up the work anyway, but with one person basically calling the shots, we won't step on each other's toes or duplicate our efforts.

"I see three paths for us to take, actually four," I say. "One is that Chris Vogel was the target, and Kim Baskin just got caught up in it because she was with him. Maybe there were things in his life that he did, or people he associated with, that put him in danger. I'll dig into that.

"The same is true for Kim Baskin: it could be that a killer was after her, and that Vogel was collateral damage. Laurie, you take her."

"Okay . . . good," Laurie says.

"The third possibility is that they were in the wrong place at the wrong time and got mixed up in something that had nothing to do with them. Or maybe it was a random killing, thrill seekers, and they weren't targeted at all.

"Marcus, you use your street connections to see if anyone knows anything and is willing to talk about it. Maybe after all these years someone might be less afraid to say what they know. Okay?"

Marcus nods and mutters something unintelligible, but I certainly take it as his agreeing with the approach.

"You said that there were four paths we could take," Laurie points out.

"Right. They could be alive and running a bed-and-breakfast in Vermont. Just because they are presumed dead, it doesn't mean they are. When there's no body, anything is possible. But it's a major long shot; I am only suggesting we consider it because we should be checking everything."

"We can resend a missing persons notice to all departments in the US; that hasn't been done in years."

I nod. "We should do that; not likely to draw a reaction, but you never know. And run credit checks to see if their names pop up anywhere."

"Right."

"And run the DNA. They have it for Vogel and Baskin; maybe it's shown up in some other jurisdiction or on one of those ancestry websites since then. It's a crazy long shot, but can't hurt."

"All of that is going to take time," Laurie says. "The department is always backed up on these kind of computer requests anyway, and we're not going to be a priority."

She's got a point. Actual cops are going to get faster treatment by the department computer people; it's just the nature of the beast. "Let's give it to them anyway, but also we can have Sam work on the credit card stuff."

She smiles. Sam Willis is Andy's accountant, but also a member of his team, in that Sam's a computer wizard who can hack into anything. Since such access is often illegal, I used to resist employing him. But his speed and accuracy have proven irresistible, so I've caved on that.

Anything that Sam gets with his unconventional methods we can always get later with a subpoena if we need it, but using him saves a hell of a lot of time.

I've come to accept Andy's view of it as "no harm, no foul," even though the cop in me knows that it really is a foul.

We're ready to start, but it's a steep hill. There's a reason this case was never solved: there simply was nothing concrete to go on.

IN MY OPINION, THE LEAD INVESTIGATORS ON THE CASE DID NOT COVER themselves in glory.

I don't generally think things like that, and I almost never say them. I tend to give cops the benefit of the doubt. I know how tough the job can be; if I went back over my cases, I would probably cringe at the mistakes I made and the things I missed. There are always too many cases and too little time.

But my sense from reading through the investigative materials, though I haven't yet gone through them in detail, is that it took a while for the detectives to accept that there was foul play. I think that was a mistake; the abandoned car should have been a flashing warning light.

By the time they realized that something awful likely happened, if they ever fully did, what little trail there was would have gotten cold.

It remains cold to this day.

The two detectives on the case were Lieutenant Joseph Olsen and Sergeant Michael Morano. Olsen is retired and lives in North Carolina, while Morano is in his early fifties and probably eyeing retirement himself. I knew both of them, though not well, when I was on the force.

Morano was called Mikey back in the day, but outgrew it. Now everyone calls him Morano, and he calls almost everyone "asshole." Morano is not the most pleasant guy in the world, but I've always known him to be a pretty good cop.

So I'm back at the precinct again; this time I've brought Simon along with me. Simon probably has more friends on the force than I do, no doubt because he has a better personality. It takes twice as long as it should for me to get back to where Morano is waiting for me, simply because Simon has to repeatedly stop to receive petting from his old friends. He's got a smile on his face and is loving the attention.

When I finally reach Morano, he says, "What, did you get lost?"

"Simon has many admirers."

"How you been?" He says it grudgingly, in keeping with his personality.

"Living the high life. You?"

"Going day by day. So, you coming in to be the hero?"

"Not how I'd phrase it. We've been assigned to take a fresh look at a cold case."

He nods. "Stanton told me to talk to you, so I'm talking to you. But everything I know is in the murder book."

"I've read it. Tell me what you don't know, but what you think."

"I think you can put your white horse back in the barn

because you're not going to come out of this with your name in lights. We didn't make any mistakes."

He keeps frowning and shifting around in his chair, like he can't wait for this meeting to end, which is too bad for him. "Look, Morano, we're just working the job. That's all. Nobody's trying to be a hero, and certainly nobody's trying to make you look bad. So just tell me what you think. Are they alive or dead?"

He looks at me and hesitates, as if trying to decide what to say. "Alive."

"Why?"

"Because if they were dead, we wouldn't have had to look for them. The bodies would have been found long ago."

"Why do you say that?"

"Because why bother to hide the bodies? Random killers wouldn't do that. If it was a drug deal gone bad, they wouldn't do that either. Bodies are not that easy to hide; why bother trying?" Morano is referring to drugs because there is some evidence that Vogel was a user.

"What about the car?"

He nods. "Makes my point for me. Why hide the bodies and leave the car with a goddamn neon light on it? If killers wanted to conceal the fact that they were dead by hiding the bodies, why do that? The car screams foul play, which is what they wanted us to think."

"Maybe it screams foul play because that's what it was."

"I don't think so. I think they ran away and abandoned the car to throw us off. Maybe they planned to come back someday but then decided the new life was better than the old one. I've considered it myself, but I'd screw up the second life the same way I screwed up this one."

I'm not buying it. "So they're about to start that new life, but go to a party first? They wanted to find courage in the punch bowl? It all sounds pretty spur-of-the-moment to me. And people who go to a reunion are usually trying to connect to their old life. That's basically the definition of reunion."

"You asked what I think. That's what I think."

"I didn't see any evidence that they were having an affair."

"You do realize that people having affairs try to keep it to themselves? Look, we turned over every rock we found, but there was nothing under them. Nobody should have wanted to kill them, and if they were just picked at random, we would have found the bodies."

"While you were turning over those rocks, did you find anything to suggest they had the kind of relationship that might result in them walking away together for the rest of their lives?" The bottom line is that I don't think there's any real chance that they are alive.

"No, but you're getting paid to find some new rocks to turn over."

"Okay. Thanks for talking to me."

"We did a good job on this."

"I know; you mentioned that already. No one is accusing you of anything."

"They'll turn up someday, but only if they want to. Or maybe they won't. But they don't want to be found. This ain't a murder case."

"I hope you're right."

"But you don't think so?"

"No. I don't."

The walk from Morano's office back to the front of the building takes twice as long as it did before. The word had apparently gotten out that Simon was in the building, so everyone who hadn't already said hello is lining the route to greet him.

He's strutting along like the grand marshal in the Rose Bowl parade. A few of his admirers take the time to grunt or nod at me, which I deeply appreciate.

I USED TO THINK OF MYSELF AS A GOOD BASKETBALL PLAYER.

I played high school ball for Eastside, and we always had one of the better teams in the state. I was a shooting guard, and in my senior year I made second team all-conference. Colleges weren't fighting over me, but I still thought I was pretty damn good, and I have the press clippings to prove it. Did I mention the time that I scored twenty-six points against Passaic?

Unfortunately, to quote the song lyrics, "that was yesterday, and yesterday's gone."

I had knee surgery about six years ago when I tore an ACL chasing some punk, but I can't blame that for my descent into basketball ordinariness. It's more a general aging and deterioration, which I can most clearly feel when I try to go to the rim. It seems like the damn basket gets higher every year, while coincidentally my jumping ability decreases.

I used to be able to dunk. Now when I jump, you could

barely slide a piece of paper under my sneakers, although I don't know why you'd want to.

Fortunately, the guys I play against these days aren't exactly entering their prime years either. They're mostly friends I played with in high school, plus a few cops I know from my days on the force. Few NBA scouts come by to watch our games.

We play behind School 20, a grammar school on the east side of town. We play on Saturdays when the kids are not around, which is probably wise, since a bunch of seventh and eighth graders could probably stop by and kick our collective ancient asses.

I'm not sure what the altitude is there; Paterson has never been referred to as the Mile High City. But based on the gasping, there seems to be much less oxygen in this area than there used to be.

I considered not playing this week; usually when I'm on a case, I focus on it full-time. But there's no time crunch; Vogel and Baskin have been missing for seven years. They're not tied to a railroad track somewhere, desperately waiting to be rescued.

So Laurie, Marcus, and I will put full effort into solving the case, but there's no ticking clock to race against, so I think it's okay to spend a couple of hours embarrassing myself on the basketball court.

It turns out not to be a great choice. I hit the first shot I take and then miss at least the next ten. Our team gets killed, and I am the major contributor to the disaster.

When we're done and are finished catching our breath, I approach probably my closest friend in the group, Barry Immerman. Barry and I graduated high school together; he went on to med school and became a doctor. He's become a valuable guy to have in these games, just in case one of us old guys has a heart attack. If Barry himself has one, he's pretty much out of luck.

"Do you remember Chris Vogel and Kim Baskin?"

"Duh." That's his way of telling me that everyone remembers them because of what transpired. Then, "Why? Are you trying to find out what happened to them?"

I nod, since the assignment is not a secret. "How well did you know them?"

"I didn't really know Kim at all, but Chris was in some of my science classes. Smart guy, but a little weird."

"Weird how?"

"I can't put my finger on it . . . just weird. He had all these theories about stuff. Always trying to convince me about some point of view he had. I didn't care about any of it, so I mostly ignored him. Gina Mancini was in that class, so I tended to focus on her."

"Everybody focused on Gina. I wonder where she is these days."

"Don't know. You were asking about Vogel?"

"Right. Who were his close friends?"

"I have no idea," Barry says. "Do you still have your yearbook?"

"I think so; in the attic. Why?"

"People listed their best friends under their photos, or at least the kids they hung out with. You could check that out; if you can't find your yearbook, I have a copy."

"Good idea."

"You think they're alive somewhere?"

I don't want to discuss my view of the case with him, so I answer with a noncommittal "Your guess is as good as mine."

"After you're done finding them, maybe you can look for your jump shot."

Ouch.

"YOU WERE CUTE, IN A GAWKY, AWKWARD, PATHETIC KIND OF WAY."

Dani is looking over my shoulder as I go through my high school yearbook, and we've arrived on the page with my photo.

"Thanks. That's high praise. I should point out that this was a particularly bad picture of me."

She smiles. "Just calling them like I see them."

"It made me look more gawky, awkward, and pathetic than I actually was."

"I can see that."

"So you wouldn't have gone out with me back then?"

"Maybe if I lost a bet. Gawky, awkward, and pathetic was never really my thing."

"I happened to do pretty well with girls. I had my pick."

"Really?"

"Maybe that's overstating it somewhat. But I did okay." Then, "I outgrew the gawky, pathetic thing, right?"

"I'm still here, aren't I?"

She points to the nickname they list for me under my photo. "Dougie? That was your nickname?"

"Right. Corey Douglas . . . Dougie."

She laughs. "I picked up on that. I guess nicknames were not that creative back in your day." I'm a year older than Dani, which she never lets me forget. She often refers to my "day," as if that were prehistoric times.

I turn to the page with Kim Baskin's photo; her nickname is listed as Kimmie. She doesn't look that familiar to me; at least, that's not how I remember her.

"She was pretty," Dani says. Then, "Should I say *was* or *is*? She might still be alive, right?"

"I'm afraid *was* is your best bet."

"You don't think she's alive?"

I shake my head. "No."

"Well, I hope she is."

I write down the names Kim listed as her best friends. They are Barb, Deb, Marcy, and Lynn. Later I'll go through the book in detail and try to figure out who exactly she is referring to. Hopefully they've listed Kim as being among their best friends, which will make the process easier. Then I'll give whatever I've come up with to Laurie for her to check it out.

Then I turn to Chris Vogel's page.

"Now, he was cute." Dani looks at the nickname. "Why did they call him Chance?"

"I have no idea."

The yearbook lists him as having been in the chemistry, physics, chess, and philosophy clubs. I didn't even know those things existed.

"Smart guy?"

"I guess so. We didn't hang out in the same clubs, that's for sure."

Vogel listed his friends as Harold, Will, and Bruce. Off the top of my head I don't know who those people are; our graduating class had eight hundred kids in it, and I wasn't the most sociable guy around. I was basically focused on sports.

But I will use the yearbook to figure out who they are and talk to them.

In most or all of the interviews that we will be conducting, we'll be going over ground that the cops covered years ago. We have existing interview reports to read, and we probably won't learn anything new. Still, it helps for us to get a sense of things ourselves.

The intervening years, while obviously not ordinarily helpful to accurate memory, can sometimes have a positive effect. Looking back, people might recall something that they might not have thought about back then, and maybe, if we ask our questions in the right way, we can jar something that they haven't mentioned before.

It's a long shot, but that's why these cases have gone cold.

Dani, having mocked my high school appearance to the extent that she can, goes off to ride the stationary bike. She does that pretty much every day. I avoid it like the plague, which is probably why I gasp for air when I play basketball.

I go back through the yearbook to identify the friends that Vogel and Baskin listed. It's not that difficult to do, and I enjoy skimming through the book and letting it jog long-ago memories.

I'm also comforted by how pretty much every guy in the class looked gawky and awkward.

I fit right in.

TODAY THE K TEAM GOES TO THE MOVIES.

We're not at a movie theater, so the popcorn is the microwave kind, which means it isn't necessary to take out a mortgage to afford it. We're at Laurie's, and we're watching video that the police collected as part of the original investigation years ago.

Almost all the footage is from the reunion, taken by attendees. Clearly Steven Spielberg was not one of those attendees; a lot of the footage is unfocused and off-center.

But there is plenty of it. Since the advent of the iPhone, people seem to think it is more important, and maybe more fun, to photograph and record life rather than actually live it. I see that as unfortunate for them, but it has definitely been a boon to police investigations everywhere.

In addition to Laurie, Marcus, and me, Dani and Andy are also settling in to watch the show. Dani is here because she is the only one of the five of us who is not a technological moron. The footage is on some kind of a drive the size of half my finger, and she knows how to miraculously get it to appear on a big-screen TV.

Andy is here because, having gone to Eastside himself, he knows many of the people in the video, and because it's morning, so there aren't any college or professional sports for him to watch.

We start the footage, which is just random stuff. According to the police records, they've done as good a job as they can to put things in chronological order, though there is no way to know from what we have what time the various videos were taken. The video is even more boring than I remember the event being.

I cringe when I see myself. I look okay, and that's the problem. The small spare tire that I currently have around my waist does not exist in this video, which may further explain the basketball exhaustion and inability to jump. I either need to get in better shape or not be so concerned with how I look. I'll probably go with the latter.

"That's Kim Baskin," Laurie says, about five minutes in. Kim's sitting at a table with three women and two men, and they are all waving to the iPhone camera. There's no way to know who is taking the video, but Chris Vogel is not one of the people at the table with Baskin. And Baskin does not betray any nervousness or sign that the next few hours are going to change her life, or end it.

It's a full ten minutes later that we see Vogel for the first time. He's at the bar, having a drink and talking in a group of four guys. I recognize the other three, two of whom were on Vogel's list of yearbook best friends. They are Harold Collison and Bruce Sharperson.

Everybody is smiling and apparently having a good time; there is no reason to think that anything serious is being discussed. And no reason to think that one of them, Chris Vogel, was planning to disappear from the known planet in a couple of hours.

There is much more video of Baskin than there is of Vogel.

She spent most of the evening with women, which makes sense, since at a reunion one usually hangs out with close friends.

Laurie and I make it into the videos a few times, but only briefly. Laurie looks like she is having fun, while I look like I'm about to fall asleep, which is basically how I remember the party.

We're disappointed when we get to the end of the footage because at no time were Vogel and Baskin shown together. If they spent any significant time with each other during the night, the prying photographers missed it. There is no clue here as to why they left together, if they did. It's impossible to determine from this video that they even knew each other.

Altogether we watch almost three hours of video. Dani leaves halfway through to go play with the dogs. Marcus, though he went to Kennedy High School and therefore doesn't know these people at all, makes it all the way through without dozing off, though I think Marcus can sleep with his eyes open.

When we're finished, Andy says, "They both seem to have left early."

I nod. "I noticed that. In the last third, there were a bunch of shots of the people they had been hanging out with most of the night, but they weren't included."

"A couple of witnesses reported them as having left together, but didn't know what time," Laurie says. "But nothing we saw indicates that they were with each other during the night. If they were leaving together to go somewhere, it's as if they had planned it in advance and didn't want to make it obvious."

"Two people planning to run off and disappear forever don't decide to spend three boring hours at a reunion first," I say. "They did not look like people about to make the most important decision of their lives."

"I'd be very surprised if they are alive," Andy says.

"I agree," I say. "I don't think we should waste any time

I ALWAYS FIND IT HELPFUL TO VISIT THE SCENE OF THE CRIME.

That's a bit difficult in this case, since we can't be sure where it is.

I drive to the hotel where the reunion took place, park, and go inside. I've got Simon with me; I find that people are much less likely to approach and annoy me when he's by my side. Simon does not have a cuddly "Oh, can I pet him?" kind of look. He's a cop, like me, and he can sneer with the best of us.

We walk through the lobby and back to the ballroom where the event was held. I don't remember it particularly well, but that's because nothing distinguishes it. It's a nice place, a good room in which to hold a reunion, as long as they bring in enough balloons.

We came in through the front door, but I notice an exit door from the ballroom to the back, where most of the cars that night were parked. Vogel and Baskin were reported as having gone through the front when they left, but someone might have slipped out that back door and been waiting for them when they walked around and reached Vogel's car.

There isn't much to be learned here, and I certainly don't learn it. Simon and I leave and drive to the rest area off the Garden State Parkway where Vogel's car was found, so that I can continue to learn nothing.

The area is just three miles from the hotel. It consists of a single building with restrooms, and a few vending machines. I have no idea if those machines were here back then, though I suspect the police photographs can enlighten me about that should I ever care to confirm. But no one drives three miles away from a party and then stops to get a soda and some pretzels.

Unless Vogel or Baskin was hit by a remarkably sudden case of food poisoning, there would be no obvious reason for them to stop here at all. It wouldn't have taken them more than five minutes to get here from the hotel; if one of them needed to go to the bathroom, it seems likely they would have done so before they left.

They either stopped here willingly or were forced to, but either way their reason for stopping had to be related to their ultimate disappearance. If they were forced to stop, it must mean that someone else was in the car with them. The only place that person could have entered the car would have been the hotel parking lot.

I suppose it's remotely possible that they stopped here for some sexual activity, but that fails the credibility test as well. I know the reunion was related to high school, but these were not teenagers. If they wanted time to themselves for that purpose, they could have gone to one of their homes or taken a room at the hotel. It could have been done without anyone finding out.

I give Simon some water and time to piss in the rest area, which seems appropriate. We then head back home so I can examine the forensic reports from the car. I'm sure there were no suspicious fingerprints; I would know that by now if there were. But I'd like to see the forensics anyway, as well as see the inventory from the car.

Dani's not home when we get there; I assume she is out doing some job-related thing. She's an event planner for mostly corporate functions, and fortunately she is able to do a lot of the job remotely. So she's home a lot, but this is not one of those times.

I'm struck that I am disappointed she's not here. In my previous, pre-Dani life, I would have been delighted to spend as much time as possible alone.

I find the documents relating to the examination of the car. Four sets of identifiable fingerprints were found. Two of them were Vogel's and Baskin's. His were everywhere, while hers were on the door by the passenger seat and the outside handle on the passenger side, which would be expected. The other two belonged to a mechanic who worked on the car, and a neighbor who had recently borrowed it. Neither rose to the level of a suspect or even a person of interest.

In addition to the typical things that would normally be found in a glove compartment, like registration, insurance card, and a car manual, there was also a clear gallon freezer bag, taped shut, which included a playing card, the king of clubs. Neither the bag nor playing card had fingerprints on them, which is suspicious. If the police came up with an explanation for this, I don't see it.

The police did the right thing and entered the information about the king of clubs into the NCIC, which is the National Crime Information Center. It's a computerized index of criminal information, which would in this case have kicked back a match if the same clue was found in connection with a crime committed anywhere in the country.

Nothing turned up.

In the back of the car was some unopened mail; Vogel might have picked it up from his mailbox on the way to the reunion. None of the mail seemed in any way significant. There was also an unopened bottle of windshield-wiper fluid and an ice scraper, unnecessary since the reunion was in May.

The trunk had three empty supermarket shopping bags, the reusable kind, a squash racquet, and an unopened can of balls.

Other than the fingerprints, nothing of Baskin's was in the car. Wherever she went when she left, she took her purse and possessions with her.

Everything I see tells me that this was not a self-planned disappearance. I don't believe there's a chance in hell that Chris Vogel and Kim Baskin are alive.

JANICE PROFAR NEEDED THESE EVENINGS.

Once a week, sometimes twice if things were awful at work, she and her coworkers would go out to drink and vent about the "idiots" that they worked for at the hospital. The more they drank, the more they vented.

They all worked in the administrative area, Janice in billing, so they never had to interact with any sick patients. The bosses, Janice and her colleagues felt, were more than sick enough to fill that gap.

Usually a dozen people gathered at McMaster's, a bar in downtown Detroit, to trade horror stories and commiserate. The conversation and the laughs, coupled with the alcohol, helped to ease the pain somewhat and to prepare everyone for another day in the office.

The regulars included nine women and three men, though the actual group members changed as people left for better jobs.

Their replacements soon came to share the disdain for management and willingly joined the group, though their time in the job might also be limited.

In this thoroughly disgruntled group, the members generally found that by banding together they could deal with anything.

Janice had worked at the hospital for three years, which put her in second place in seniority in the group. She was contemplating leaving. She had signed on to one of those online job placement services and had recently gone on a few unsuccessful interviews. She was a finalist in the last case, so she felt like her time was coming.

Her best friend at work, Rita Laureano, had been sober for three years, so that made her the perfect designated driver. Janice marveled at how Rita could watch them all get blasted and not give in to temptation and respected her friend's discipline. On more than one occasion Janice had asked Rita if it would be better for her if Janice didn't drink, but Rita said that it didn't matter, that she had made a commitment to herself that she was going to keep.

On this particular night, Rita drove three of the group to their homes at around eleven o'clock. Janice was the last to be dropped off, which means that Rita was the last person known to have seen her alive.

She was strangled, and the time of death was thought to be before midnight, which means her killer was likely in place and waiting for her when she got home.

In the four years since, no one had come up with any idea as to who killed Janice Profar, or why.

And no one knows that the last words she heard were "four of diamonds."

IT'S HARD TO COME UP WITH SOMETHING REALLY BAD TO SAY ABOUT Rutgers.

The state university of New Jersey, it provides an outstanding education to almost seventy thousand undergraduate and graduate students annually at a comparatively reasonable price, especially for New Jersey residents.

The campuses are quite impressive, especially the main one in East Brunswick, where I am today. It a beautiful early May day, and students are out and about, reading and talking and throwing Frisbees and doing student stuff. Looks like a nice life; maybe I should have gone to college.

Of course, since I can say something bad about pretty much anything, I choose to focus on the sports situation at Rutgers. Some genius decided that they deserved to be a big-time program, so they entered the Big Ten. It's roughly comparable to me waking up tomorrow and deciding I want to go one-on-one with LeBron James.

It's fair to say that the football coaches at Ohio State and Michigan did not react by screaming, *"Oh, my God! Rutgers is coming! Whatever will we do?"* What they wound up doing, and continue to do, is beating Rutgers like a drum, no matter how much money Rutgers puts into their program.

The average professor's salary at Rutgers is $172,000. Not bad, but the football coach makes $4 million. So far, the professors win almost as many games and, I'm sure, commit fewer recruiting violations.

Not that my heart is breaking for the professors. Believe me, the cop they would call if someone was pointing a gun at them makes a lot less than they do. I'm just saying that our educational priorities may be a bit off-kilter.

I'm here to talk with one of those professors today, Bruce Sharperson, one of the friends that Vogel listed in the yearbook. Sharperson is also one of the people that spent some time talking to Vogel at the reunion, as shown in the video.

I didn't know Sharperson in high school. You could say that we had a nodding acquaintance, but as I recall, we didn't nod much back then. He's a psychology professor now, which indicates we probably didn't have that much in common. There was a greater likelihood that I would become a Martian hairdresser than a psychology professor.

I've googled him to get any advance information that I can, and I'm surprised to see that he is the son of Andrew Sharperson, a major player in the venture capital world. Andrew died eleven years ago and was obviously rich. If Bruce inherited it, then it certainly explains why he can get by with less than the football coach.

When I get to his office, the one assistant seems to cover

all six professors listed in the directory. "Professor Sharperson should be back any minute," she says. "His class is just letting out now. Is he expecting you?"

"He is."

"You could wait in his office if you'd like. You'll be more comfortable in there."

I accept the offer and go into a small office that can't be more than fifteen feet square. Bookshelves cover every wall, most of their books having to do with various areas of psychology. It is amazing how many books have been written that I have never read, or heard of.

It probably makes sense that I didn't go to college, even though I can handle a Frisbee with the best of them.

The door opens and Professor Sharperson comes in. He's a bit unkempt, in a professorial sort of way, but smiles and offers his hand. "Corey? Don't take this the wrong way, but did we know each other in high school?"

I return the smile. "I've been trying to figure that out myself. I guess it's fair to say that if we did, we weren't particularly close."

"Probably true."

"What class were you just teaching?"

"Predictive theory."

"What does that mean?"

"Do you really want to know?"

"Tell me the CliffsNotes version."

He smiles. "Hard to do, but I'll try. Rational humans behave in entirely predictable ways, one hundred percent of the time. That has developed over time in its own form of evolution. But it can be incredibly limiting."

"How so?"

"Well, for example, you as a policeman are among the most predictable of people. You have been trained that way. But your adversaries, if they are smart enough, can develop an under-standing of what you are planning to do, and it could help them counter it."

"Like the shift in baseball."

"I'm not familiar with that."

"Teams use analytics to position their defensive players. For example, if a right-handed hitter pulls the ball most of the time, they will put three players on that side of the infield."

He shakes his head. "Not exactly. You're confusing what peo-ple will likely do with what they want to do. Though both are important in their own way."

"So you are teaching your students to be unpredictable?"

"I'm teaching them that everyone is predictable. Understand-ing that is what is important in dealing with many aspects of life and interpersonal relationships." Then, "You wanted to talk about Chris Vogel?"

"Yes."

"May I ask why?"

"Some colleagues and I are investigating the case again, try-ing to see if a fresh look might help."

"Are your efforts sanctioned by the police?"

"They are."

"Commendable diligence; it's been quite a few years. So how can I help?"

"He was a close friend of yours?"

He nods. "If you're talking about our high school days, then, yes, he was. Which I confess made him somewhat unique back then."

"You didn't have a lot of friends?"

"A select group." Sharperson smiles. "We were the ones who did not attend the football games on Saturday. I assume you didn't notice that we weren't there?"

"Afraid not; I was playing. You and Chris shared the same interests?"

"I suppose so; who can remember back that far? We were definitely in some of the same clubs."

"Had you maintained the friendship in the years leading up to the reunion?"

"Not really. We were occasionally in touch, but it lessened over time."

"The night of the reunion, did you speak with him much?"

"Yes, I believe I did. People tend to revert to old behavior at those kind of events. It's an odd dynamic."

"Is that one of your predictive theories?"

He smiles. "Yes, I suppose it is. It certainly doesn't come from observation; that was my first and most definitely last reunion."

"Did you notice anything unusual about him? Did he seem nervous, anxious, excited?"

"I thought about that night a great deal, after what happened. But he seemed perfectly normal; the night seemed not to have a special significance for him, at least not that he betrayed. But we weren't friends at that point, so he would not have opened up to me."

"Had he ever talked about Kim Baskin? Was there a relationship between them that you were aware of?

"No, but you should not view that as significant. In high school no one in our small group was particularly successful with women." Sharperson smiles. "The plight of the nerds. And after that we weren't close enough that I would have been aware of his romantic relationships. But I don't believe he mentioned Ms. Baskin that night. I remember being surprised when someone said they had left together."

"Any serious enemies you knew about?" The police have asked all these questions of everyone, including Sharperson, and they've been answered, but sometimes it helps me to ask them again, and to hear the answers myself.

"None that I was aware of, but fifteen years is plenty of time to accumulate enemies as well as friends."

"Did he strike you as the type to intentionally disappear? To start a new life?"

"No. But . . ." Sharperson hesitates. "Chris had developed some habits which Harold and I did not share."

He's talking about Harold Collison, another friend listed in the yearbook, and part of the small group that the reunion videos showed spent time together that night. "Habits?"

"There was said to be some drug use. Nothing I ever witnessed; I want to make that clear. And gambling. Again, these are just things I heard, but they probably had some causal effect on his separating from Harold and me in the years after we graduated."

"He was a gambler?"

"That was the prevailing view."

"Is that why his nickname was Chance?"

Sharperson looks surprised. "I had never heard that. We never called Chris that."

"What did you call him?"

"Chris."

CHRIS VOGEL WAS A CAR SALESMAN.

He sold both new and used cars, and he must have been a good one, because here in the office of his former boss a plaque lists the Salesman of the Year for the past twenty-five years. Chris received the honor four times, and I assume it would have been more had he been around the last seven years to be in the competition.

Chris's boss, or at least the current manager of the dealership, is Peter Hauser. He asked me to wait for him in his glass-enclosed office, and from here I can see him consulting with one of his salesmen, who has just left a potential car-buying couple in his own office while he and Hauser have their conversation.

I'm sure they are pretending to discuss just how fantastic a deal they can give the buyers. Based on my experience in similar situations, it will probably result in them throwing in nonexistent undercoating.

Has anyone ever seen an undercoating factory or knows anyone who worked in one? Do you know anyone who has said, "Whew . . . I dodged a bullet that time, I'm sure glad I had that undercoating"? And if undercoating works so well, why don't they also sell overcoating?

The conversation finishes and Hauser heads back toward me, while the salesman returns to his office to close the sale. "So, Mr. Douglas, what can I do for you?"

I point back to where they were just talking. "Did you throw in the undercoating?"

He laughs. "We might have. I leave that up to the discretion of the salesperson. They each have their own style, within assigned parameters. The process works better that way."

"Did Chris Vogel have a good style?"

"As good as I've ever seen. Are you here to talk about Chris?"

"Yes, I'm investigating the case."

"Any progress on finding his killer?"

"Not to my knowledge."

Hauser shakes his head. "Still hard to believe, all these years later."

"Based on his awards and your comment about his style, he was a good salesman?"

"Outstanding. Better than me, and I could get you to buy a car right now."

"That would be a neat trick."

He smiles. "I'll even throw in the undercoating."

"Now you're talking. So why was he so good?"

"Because he didn't give a shit."

"I don't understand."

"I'm sure he wanted to close the sales. I mean that's why he came to work, and that's how he made money. But he had some kind of . . . I don't know . . . Zen? . . . attitude about it. Like whatever was going to happen was going to happen."

"Like it was preordained?"

"Not exactly. I mean, it wasn't about God or some spiritual thing. It was like he was doing what he could, and then what would be, would be. It was a terrible attitude for a salesman, but customers responded to it, and I wish all my people had it the way he did."

"Did you socialize with him outside of work?"

A firm shake of the head. "I don't ever do that with my sales-people; I never want to have to fire a friend. But I sure as hell wouldn't have done it with Chris."

"Why not?"

"He was strange. Nothing about him would surprise me, so I never tried to find out."

"Did he take drugs?"

Hauser's attitude immediately becomes wary. "I never saw anything. I had suspicions, but that's all. That doesn't cut it here, but I can't do anything without knowing for sure. And he always seemed clearheaded and in control at work. What he does away from work is not my business."

"Did his going missing surprise you?"

"Going missing? I thought he was murdered."

"Probably was. But if you found out that he just disappeared, voluntarily, would that have surprised you?" I ask this question not because I think the disappearance was voluntary, but rather as a way to get insight into Vogel's way of thinking.

"Yeah, but with Chris less than most. Like I say, he was a strange one."

"Strange enough to make some bad enemies?"

"Not that I know of, but that doesn't mean anything. The

truth is, I didn't know that much about Chris. I doubt too many people did."

"Was he a gambler?"

Hauser shrugs. "Again, I don't know, so I'm the wrong guy to ask."

"Did you know Kim Baskin?"

"Never met her and never heard Chris mention her. I don't think I ever heard Chris mention any woman."

"Anything else about Chris that stands out?"

Hauser thinks for a few moments. "He was smart. I mean really smart. He knew a lot about everything; it was amazing. And then he put it into these theories of life that he'd go on about; half the time I never knew what he was talking about. Make that ninety percent of the time. He was way too smart to work here; he could have been doing more important stuff."

"Did he ever talk about high school?"

Hauser laughs. "He hated high school. I went to Eastside fifteen years before him, and I loved it. He had the opposite experience."

"Did he ever say why?"

"Apparently he was not a big man on campus. Strangeness doesn't always play that well in high school."

"Were you surprised to hear he even went to a reunion if he hated it so much?"

Hauser pauses. "I hadn't thought about it, but now that you put it that way, yeah, I'm surprised he went." Then, "And the way it turned out, I'm sorry he did."

USUALLY I GO THROUGH LAURIE WHEN I NEED TO TALK TO MARCUS.

It's nothing against Marcus; I simply cannot understand his grunting noises; I have no idea what he is saying. Andy warned me about it; he said he hasn't correctly deciphered a word Marcus has said in years. If ever.

As a remarkably scary guy, he also makes Andy uncomfortable and intimidated. I don't feel that way; I've spent a lot of time around tough guys, both for me and against me. Not Marcus tough, of course, but tough. Marcus is my partner and a damn good one. We just quite literally speak different languages.

But Laurie is at some kind of event at their son Ricky's school today, and I'd like to get Marcus started on something, so I take a deep breath and call him. It should work out; I'll do all the talking. He understands me, even if I can't understand him.

He answers the phone on the first ring. "Yuhhnn?"

"Marcus, it's me, Corey."

"Hey, Corey."

Did he just say, "Hey, Corey?" And did I just understand what he said? "Marcus?"

"What?"

"This is Marcus, right?"

"Yes, you're Corey and I'm Marcus. We're set with that. What do you want?"

I don't know what to make of this; it's disorienting. "You just sound different, that's all."

"You still haven't told me what you want."

My mind is racing through the possibilities. This person answered Marcus's phone. Could someone have taken his phone? The Russian army couldn't take Marcus's phone. But how is it that he can suddenly communicate so clearly?

I'm going to assume it's Marcus, mainly because what I have to say is not top secret. If it's someone else on the call, they won't have much to gain from being privy to this information.

"Marcus, Vogel seems to have been a gambler, so maybe he was in too deep to some dangerous people. If you get a chance, can you check into that?"

"Sure."

"Sure?"

"That's what I said."

"I'm sorry, Marcus, but you sound different."

"Yeah, you already mentioned that."

"Okay, thanks."

"No problem; I'll get right on it."

I get off the phone and run through the possibilities in my head. That was either Marcus, someone who stole Marcus's phone, or an alien pod that has taken over Marcus's body.

I'm not sure an alien pod would be tough enough to pull it off, but that seems like the likeliest possibility.

"THERE'S NOTHING TO BE FOUND," SAM WILLIS SAYS.

Sam has joined us at Laurie's house to update us on what he's learned from his cyber search for signs of Vogel and Baskin since their disappearance. Based on his opening line, I have a feeling he's not about to crack the case wide open.

"No credit card activity on the existing cards, which of course have since been closed for years. No new cards applied for, or credit activity of any kind. No bank accounts, brokerage accounts, phone numbers, death certificates, anything.

"No name changes applied for, no property purchased, no driver's licenses, et cetera, et cetera, et cetera. These two people are completely off the grid, at least under these names. And it is extremely difficult in this day and age to remain off the grid."

"Can it be done?" Laurie asks.

"You mean by a CIA agent? Maybe. By a car salesman and a dental hygienist? I'd have to see it to believe it."

"I'll take that as a no," Laurie says.

"Anything else you can do?" I ask him, knowing the answer to the question as I ask it.

He shakes his head. "Sorry, not without more information. If they are alive, and if I had the names they are using, I could tell you everything you'd need to know. But without those names, I have nowhere to turn."

"Okay, thanks, Sam," Laurie says.

"If you want my opinion, these people are not among the living."

"What about the witness protection program?" Laurie asks. "Couldn't that explain their being off the grid under their real names?"

Sam thinks about it for a moment. "It's a possibility, but I can't confirm it one way or the other. Interesting, though. Did they witness anything?"

"Not that we know of," I say. "And unfortunately one of the main admission requirements for the witness protection program is to be a witness."

Sam laughs. "I've heard that. It's the first thing they ask during the interview."

Sam leaves, and Laurie updates me on her progress on the Kim Baskin side of the case. So far she has spoken to Baskin's fiancé and a close friend who was a coworker of hers at the dental practice. Both are sure they never heard Baskin mention Chris Vogel, and equally sure that she would never voluntarily disappear.

Each of them said they regretted to admit that they are positive she must be dead, or they would have heard from her long before now.

I assure Laurie that I am not getting anywhere either and update her on my efforts so far. I tell her about the rumors of Vogel's gambling and say, "I spoke to Marcus about it."

"Good."

"No, I mean I spoke to Marcus. And he spoke to me. We spoke to each other."

"I said, 'Good.'"

"Let me try to make this clearer. Marcus and I had a conversation. He understood what I was saying, and I understood what he was saying."

Laurie nods knowingly and smiles. "Ahh, welcome to the club."

"You mean you knew about this?"

"Yes. I mean, I didn't know that Marcus would show you that side, but yes."

"I don't understand."

She pauses before she answers. "Marcus takes advantage of people not being able to communicate with him; he uses it to his advantage. So that's what he shows pretty much everyone until he fully trusts them. He obviously has come to trust you, which I am pleased about, since we're all on the same team."

"And Andy? He doesn't trust Andy?"

"That's a special case. Yes, I believe he trusts Andy. But he also knows he scares the hell out of Andy, so I think he's playing a game. At one point I was going to ask him to stop, but nothing is really harmed, so I'm just letting Marcus be Marcus."

"So I shouldn't tell Andy the truth?"

"I'm married to him, and I haven't. I'd rather keep something from Andy than upset Marcus."

"Good point. Me too."

LARRY VENEGAS IS UNIQUE IN AT LEAST ONE RESPECT.

He is the only person who admitted to the police that he was a friend of Chris Vogel's at the time of his disappearance. Actually, he's one of two, but he's the only one who is still alive. The other one died of cancer at the age of fifty-three two years ago.

Both men lived in the same garden apartment complex as Vogel, and Venegas lived right next door. He told the cops that he had no idea what happened to his friend, and I'm sure he'll say the same to me, but it's a box I need to check.

Venegas works as a bartender in Passaic. He says we can talk while he's working, as long as we do it in midafternoon, around 4:00 P.M. According to him, there will be few customers at that time, and those who will be there will have been drinking since lunch and will be semicoherent and quite incapable of overhearing us.

The place is somewhere between ordinary and a dump. Some

bars deliberately have sawdust on the floor for ambience; this one has it because the wood floors are so old that they are fraying. Of course, there are two pinball machines, a bumper pool table, and three televisions showing ESPN, so it's not all bad.

Venegas is alone behind the bar, which is easily sufficient, since only three customers are in the place. If you find yourself in this establishment at 4:00 P.M. on a beautiful spring afternoon like today, it might be time to reassess your situation.

As Venegas predicted, the three customers do not seem to be on the alert side at this point.

"I told the cops all I knew back when Vogel took off" is his opening salvo. "And it wasn't much."

"You think he took off? Meaning he left on his own?"

"Yeah."

"Why?"

"Because that was Chris. Whatever you thought he would do, he'd do the opposite. You could never tell what he was going to do, or what he really had on his mind."

"So in the weeks before he 'took off,' he didn't seem worried about anything? Didn't talk about any enemies he might have?"

"Nah. But he was using pretty heavily then."

"Cocaine?"

Venegas nods. "Yeah. That's another reason I think he left. He could have decided to go clean and get away for a fresh start."

"Did he ever talk about that?"

"Not to me."

"Do you know where he was getting the drugs?"

"No. That's not my thing, you know? Never was."

"Chris was a gambler too, wasn't he?"

Venegas surprises me with a big laugh. "Yeah, you can say that. The guy would bet on anything." He points to the other customers. "If he was here now, he'd bet on which one of these guys would pass out first."

"I'll take the guy sitting in the corner."

Venegas shakes his head. "Nah, you'd lose. He's a regular. Never passes out; just sits there and drinks until he leaves. Walks a straight line; I think he's got a hollow leg."

"Was Chris a successful gambler?"

"No such thing, man. No such thing. But the thing about Chris was he didn't care which side he took. Giants are playing the Eagles? He'd tell you to take a side, and he'd take the other one. The point spread makes it an even game, so he didn't care which side he was on. He figured there's no way to predict, so he just wanted the action."

"Did he gamble on sports?"

"Sports, blackjack, craps, the weather . . . I'm telling you, the guy would bet on anything."

"What about girlfriends?"

Venegas shakes his head. "Can't help you there. He never mentioned one, and I never saw him with one. I would say he could have gone in the other direction, but I never saw him with a guy either."

"So you never heard the name Kim Baskin until she disappeared with him?"

"Right."

I thank him for his help and take a quick look at the guy in the corner before I leave. I still think he's going to be the first one to have his head hit the table, but I don't want to stay around to confirm it.

Once I'm in the car, my cell phone rings.

It's Laurie. "Can you come by? Marcus is here and has something for us."

I STILL CAN'T GET USED TO UNDERSTANDING MARCUS.

Out of habit, I find myself involuntarily straining to understand what he says, even though it is perfectly clear. It is like looking for English subtitles in a movie that is in English.

Marcus updates us on what he's learned so far, which focuses on Vogel's gambling habit. Andy's not around, so there is no need to decipher grunts or find out the information through Laurie. Marcus just talks normally, which still feels abnormal.

I'm flattered that Marcus has taken me into his confidence, at least as it relates to this. It means that he considers me a trusted friend. I wish I could lord it over Andy by telling him what's going on, but if I did, Marcus would probably beat me, his good buddy, to death.

The news he has to convey is not great. Vogel was indeed a big gambler, probably beyond his means. At the time of his death he owed considerable money, though Marcus has not been able to find out how much.

That's not the bad news. The bad news is that the bookmaker he owed the money to is Anthony Velasco.

There are two types of bookmakers in this area. One is the small-time guy . . . and it's always *guy*. . . . I am personally unaware of any female bookmakers, though I guess they may exist.

The small-timer is always a semi-independent contractor who works with the permission of Joseph Russo, Jr., the head of the aptly named Russo crime family. The small-timer does not handle big money, and when more comes in than he can handle, he lays it off with one of Russo's people. For the right to operate, he pays Russo a piece of the action.

The other type, the big-time guy, works for Russo directly; Russo is the absent CEO of his operation. He handles the big money players and all the profit goes to Russo, who then pays the bookie and his people, probably handsomely.

This represents a problem for us because not only would Velasco be supported by a significant amount of muscle, but to piss him off is to effectively piss off Russo as well. On the list of people there's no upside to pissing off, Russo would rank just under Vladimir Putin.

One of the questionable sides to my personality, probably worthy of the therapy I will never subject myself to, is that I like annoying people like Russo and getting them angry at me. It's one of the reasons I enjoyed being a cop, and why I like the job I have right now. It's also a major reason my life expectancy is so low.

So we need to talk to Velasco, and we assign Marcus the job of figuring out the best way to do it. That is well within Marcus's skill set, so he will let us know when he's made the plan and is ready to execute it.

In the meantime, I leave to interview Vogel's mother, Brenda

Crews. When I called her, the first thing I discovered was that she was my English teacher during my freshman year of high school. She tried unsuccessfully to teach me a love, or at least a tolerance, for poetry.

I didn't mention it to her, and she didn't show any recognition of my name. But when I told her why I was calling, she was surprisingly receptive to talking to me about her son. I had been afraid that she would view it as opening old wounds, but that didn't seem to be the case.

Miss Crews, as she was known to us, now lives in an apartment complex in Freehold called Castle Village. It's a reasonably well-kept place, but definitely showing its age.

I'm familiar with Freehold, since I misspent some of my youth going to the harness track there. My friends and I used to stop there either on the way to the shore or on the way home. For non–New Jerseyites, *shore* is the word we use for "beach."

There's no doorman at Castle Village, which is not a surprise, so I ring the buzzer and Miss Crews buzzes me up after I identify myself.

When I was in high school, I never realized that Chris Vogel was her son. Maybe she didn't want people to know that and that's why she used what is probably her maiden name. Certainly doesn't matter now.

When she opens the door, the first thing I notice is how much older and more frail she looks. She's in a wheelchair, the kind that runs on a power source and does not require manual effort to get around.

She takes one look at me, smiles, and says, "Freshman English. You sat in the back and never raised your hand. But you talked to your friends a lot."

"You remember me?" I ask, though she has already demonstrated that she does. "That's amazing."

"I wasn't sure about the name, but I never forget a face, though you were more awkward looking back then."

"So I've been told."

"I gave you a B-minus, and you were lucky to get that."

"I know."

We go into her small den, and she offers me coffee and some kind of cookies that she says she baked yesterday. They are fantastic; they taste like cherry vanilla ice cream. She seems to be staring at Simon. "What a beautiful dog."

"Stop, you'll swell his head."

"I haven't had a dog in years. And I love them. It would be wonderful to have one to take care of, and to keep me company."

I wonder if she could fully handle a dog, since she is wheelchairbound, but she responds to that without my having to delicately ask. "Mrs. Simmons next door said she would help me if I got a dog. She loves them, but her husband is allergic. We talk about it a lot; we could be coparents."

"I know someone who might be able to help you get one," I say, thinking about Andy and the dog rescue foundation he is a partner in.

"That would be wonderful. Now tell me why you're here. Is there news about Chris?"

"No."

She sighs in relief. "Good. It allows me my silly hope."

"I'm a private investigator and a retired cop. My colleagues and I are working on the case; we're employed by the police department."

"Will you tell me if you learn anything?"

"I will." I mean it sincerely. I can't think of too many things worse than a parent not knowing if their child is alive or dead.

"So how can I help?"

"I'm not sure that you can. I'm just going around asking

questions. Maybe the answers will tell me something, maybe they won't."

I ask her the typical questions I've been asking everyone, and her responses are unenlightening. For example, she never heard the name Kim Baskin and is positive that she would have if her son had had a relationship with her.

As we seem to be wrapping up, and as I finish the last of the cookies, a strange look comes over her face, as if she's wrestling with a problem or trying to make a decision.

"I need your help. Can I trust you?"

"You can. And I owe you for the B-minus."

She doesn't smile at my response; she simply wheels herself out of the room. It's a full sixty seconds before she comes back with some pieces of paper, two of which she puts down in front of me. "I found this in his apartment years ago when I finally summoned the courage to go through his things."

It's a list, in alphabetical order, of everyone who was going to attend the reunion. In looking at it more carefully, it seems to be the first page of what must have been a longer list, since it only gets as far as the names that start with C. On the page that's here, probably about fifty of the names are enclosed by a box scrawled in some kind of marker. Handwritten at the top is a note, which says, in ballpoint pen, *See you there. Fred.*

"Who's Fred?"

"He was in the class too, and on the reunion committee. I found that out afterwards."

I'm not sure what to make of this; it's not terribly unusual for someone to want to know who was going to be at a reunion before deciding whether to attend. But I don't have much time to think about it before she says, "There's something else. Read this."

She puts the other piece of paper in front of me. The bottom third of the page has been torn off, and what remains is hand-printed in what looks like ballpoint pen: *Mom. No matter what you may hear, do not worry about me. I will be fine . . . say nothing to anyone . . . until I see you.*

"When did you get this?"

"Two days before Chris left."

"What was on the piece that's been torn off?"

"Just something personal between Chris and me; nothing that relates to what happened. I eventually threw it out; it was too painful."

I have my doubts that a mother would throw away something so personal from her missing son, but I don't push it. I assume she's saying it so that I don't press her to show it to me. Maybe I will deal with it later if it becomes necessary.

"Okay. Did you show this to the police?"

"No."

"Why? Because he asked you not to?"

She nods. "Based on this, I knew he was okay; that he had reasons for leaving. I was listening to him because I was afraid that my revealing the letter would ruin whatever he was doing and might get him in trouble. I made a terrible mistake by not showing it to the police."

"So you think he's alive?"

She shakes her head in obvious sadness. "No, not anymore. Too much time has gone by; he would have contacted me. Something happened to him . . . something terrible. Whatever he was planning went horribly wrong. I've been agonizing over whether to finally show it to the police. Now I have shown it to you; please find out what happened to my son."

"I'll do my best; I can promise you that."

I STOP OFF AT LAURIE AND ANDY'S ON THE WAY HOME.

I want to tell Laurie about my meeting with Brenda Crews, but am going to do it in person because that way she can also see the note.

But mainly I want to talk to Andy.

I tell them both about my conversation and show them the letter. Then I ask Andy if Brenda can be in legal jeopardy for not having given the police the letter back when they were investigating.

"It's possible. But I would have to see a transcript of her interviews with the police back then to answer definitively."

"We have those transcripts," Laurie says.

Andy nods. "It all depends on what they asked her and how she answered. If she lied to them, meaning if she said she had not heard from Vogel and had no communication from him relating to his disappearance, then she committed an illegal act. If not, or if there is significant ambiguity about it, then she'd be fine.

"But either way it's unlikely anyone has the inclination or the stomach to prosecute the wheelchairbound mother of a murder victim, even in an unsolved case. It's not like she was doing it to protect the killer or thwart justice."

"That's what I thought, but you'll look at the transcript?"

"I will. But I also see no reason for you to share this with anyone outside of your group, at least for now. If you solve the case, and the letter becomes probative, then that will require more planning, and we can revisit it."

"Okay."

"Who should I send the bill to for my legal advice?" Andy asks.

"Laurie."

"I'll have our accountants go over it to see if it's fair," she says.

"What would be a fair charge?" Andy asks.

"Zero."

Andy shakes his head. "Seems a bit low."

Laurie asks how the letter from Vogel to his mother affects my view of the case.

"I don't know that it does. It's fairly ambiguous. It shows he knew something significant was about to happen, but while she originally read it as a sign that he had disappeared voluntarily, that's not necessarily what it means. He could have been involved with dangerous people, and that he expected things to come to a head."

Laurie nods. "And it may not have developed like he planned."

"I still think he's dead. But among the things I don't understand is what Kim Baskin had to do with this."

"Maybe he got that list of people who were going to make sure that she was going to be there," Laurie says.

"He had a bunch of names circled; her name was in that group. But if they were close enough to leave the place together, couldn't he have just asked her if she was coming?"

"I haven't talked to anyone who knew of a relationship between them," Laurie says.

"It could be that they just went off together for whatever reason, maybe a planned date, and that whatever went down happened while she was there," Andy says. "Wrong place, wrong time."

"But it makes it more likely that they are dead," Laurie says. "There is absolutely no indication that they were planning to run off, either individually and certainly not together. Andy?"

"You want more free consultation?"

"I do."

"Okay. I think you have it figured correctly. It sounds like Vogel is the person to focus on. He was the one who had contact with dangerous people, and from what Corey has learned, he was unpredictable, a bit of a loose cannon."

"So we're agreed," I say. "Any word from Marcus?"

Laurie nods. "He called a few minutes ago."

MARK TWAIN SAID, "THE REPORTS OF MY DEATH ARE GREATLY exaggerated."

He didn't intend it this way, but it's a quote that could perfectly apply to bookies.

When sports betting was legalized in the United States and adopted by most of the individual states, those not involved in gambling believed that it would be the death knell for bookies. Why would anyone bet illegally with often unsavory characters when they could just as easily make the same bet legally?

The answer can be summed up in two words: *credit* and *taxes*.

Credit is by far the most important one. Let's say you wanted to bet $1,000 on each of ten games. If you make the bets legally, you have to give $10,000 in advance of the games being played. Actually, it's $11,000 because of something called *vig*, but let's forget about that for now.

If you bet with a bookie, you don't put up anything at all; he gives you credit. Most people don't expect to lose all ten games, so they would not need to have the full $10,000 available. For example, if they have a bad day and win three of the games, losing seven, they only have to come up with $4,000.

Not having to put up all the money in advance is extremely attractive to the average gambler. It allows that person to bet much more, to have more "action" on more games. The downside is that it can lead to owing to dangerous people money that the losing gambler may not have.

People like Anthony Velasco and his boss, Joseph Russo, Jr.

Taxes enter the picture because people are generally not crazy about paying them. If one wins any reasonably significant money when betting legally, the betting entity is obligated to report the winnings to the IRS. That obviously doesn't happen with illegal wagering.

Few people win consistently, so the tax situation shouldn't matter. But one overriding thing about gamblers is that they always think they are going to win, despite years of evidence to the contrary.

The K Team is taking a field trip tonight to see and talk to Velasco. We didn't call ahead of time to make an appointment; he wouldn't have agreed to meet us, and it would have removed the element of surprise. Surprises make field trips like this more fun.

Marcus has scouted out the situation and told us that Velasco has four men that work for him every night, either as bodyguards or running errands. Their home base is an office in downtown Paterson on Van Houten Street, which is just down the block and across the street from Andy's office. Andy's place is above a fruit stand; he definitely does not blow his money on rent. But it will serve as an excellent vantage point for us on this operation.

Velasco stays in the office throughout the night while two of the men go out to make collections and pay off winners. Suffice it to say, they do more collecting than paying.

They are usually gone for a couple of hours. Then, when they return with the money, the other two men go out and finish the rounds. This way Velasco always has two men with him as protection. The switchover usually takes place around 10:00 P.M., though that can vary.

We get to Andy's office at nine thirty; it's Marcus, Laurie, Simon, and me. I like to bring Simon whenever I can to meetings that might turn unpleasant; he has certain skills that are comforting to have on my side.

We take turns sitting near the window and looking out to see when the two men return and the other two leave. Tonight that happens at a quarter after ten. We wait until the departing men have gotten in their car and driven away, then Laurie says, "Let's go."

Marcus and Laurie go around the block so that they will come from the opposite direction from Simon and me. We two walk by first, just to make sure that nothing seems out of line. Just a boy and his dog out for a nice walk.

We pass Marcus and Laurie about thirty yards past Velasco's office, and I nod that things seem okay. They continue walking toward the office. I stop, as if to let Simon do his business, though he would never consider doing so when we're working. We then turn around and walk back toward the office.

I watch Marcus and Laurie stop at the office. Laurie tries the door and sees that it's locked, which is not exactly a major deterrent to Marcus. He bends toward the door, hits it with his shoulder, and presto, it is open. Had he used his full force, the building might have come down.

Simon and I step up our pace and reach the door in about ten seconds. We go inside. Usually Simon's presence causes surprise and concern in people; he has a no-nonsense look about him that can be intimidating to suspects or people we want to scare.

I can quickly tell based on what I see that in this case further intimidation is not necessary. Anthony Velasco sits behind a desk. His two enforcers are on the floor in front of the desk; they are either unconscious or pretending to be asleep.

They must clearly have been trying to protect their boss and must have annoyed Marcus. I don't see any weapons on the floor; they were apparently attempting to take on Marcus with their bare hands. I don't know much about them, but I've got a hunch neither of them is missing a Mensa meeting to be here tonight.

"What the hell is going on?" Velasco looks more than a little worried. If we are here to kill him, nothing is now stopping us from doing so. I'm sure he is well aware of that.

I leave Simon at the door. He is outstanding at sensing the arrival of visitors. Laurie is watching the door also, but Simon will alert us if anybody approaches, well before Laurie can see anyone. And if they have bad intentions, Simon will make them regret their arrival. Anyone who comes in holding a gun will answer in the future to the nickname One Arm.

Simon is good at judging people with bad intentions. If he were human, he'd be Marcus.

"Sorry for the intrusion," I say. "Please offer our apologies to these two if and when they wake up. They look like fun guys."

"There's more where they came from," says Velasco, his tough guy persona gradually being restored.

"I think I speak for all of us when I say we are fully intimidated by the prospect. So let's not waste any time. We're here to talk about Chris Vogel."

Velasco doesn't say anything for a few moments, a puzzled look on his face. "Who?" he finally asks, and I think he legitimately can't place the name. After all, it has been seven years.

"You know who Vogel is," Laurie says. "He owed you money and then coincidentally disappeared seven years ago."

"Vogel . . . right, Vogel. I know who you mean. What about him?"

"Where did he disappear to?" I ask.

"How the hell should I know?"

"How much did he owe you?"

"I don't remember."

"How much did he owe you?" Sometimes asking a question a second time elicits a response.

This is one of those times. "Maybe twenty grand."

"So you had him killed," Laurie says.

He laughs. "For twenty grand? We don't kill people for twenty grand. Maybe they have to use a walker for a few months, but we don't kill them."

"But you were pissed off that he hadn't paid," Laurie says.

"You better believe I was pissed off. He has the money to buy drugs, he can pay his gambling debts."

"Did you cut him off? Stop taking his action?"

"Damn straight. And you know why? I'll tell you why. Your boy was talking to the Feds. I don't deal with people who do that, no matter what they're talking about. It's a character flaw."

"Was he talking to them about you?"

"Nah. Why would he talk to the narcs about me?"

"How do you know this?" Laurie asks.

"It's my business to know things."

"Then do you know what happened to him?"

"No. And to tell you the truth, I don't care." Then, "We done here?"

I BELIEVED ANTHONY VELASCO.

Not because I think he has any allegiance to the truth; I generally wouldn't trust him as far as Marcus could throw him.

I just don't believe he would have been able to make up the story about Vogel talking to federal narcotics officers in the moment; nor would he have any reason to do so. He had already denied being responsible for Vogel's disappearance; nothing we could do would compel him to say otherwise.

Gambling debts rarely get people killed, especially if the amount was really in the $20,000 range, as Velasco said. And the drug business is exponentially more dangerous. That Kim Baskin was also killed makes Velasco even less likely to have done it; for a gambling debt that is literally overkill.

Most interesting was his statement that not only was Vogel involved with drugs, but he was working with the DEA. If that is true, it would ordinarily put the witness protection program higher up on the list of possibilities for what happened to him. It would explain a lot; the mysterious disappearance, the failure to find a body, and that there has been no trace of him.

The only thing it does not explain is Kim Baskin, and that's the main reason it basically falls apart. Laurie has uncovered no information that she had anything to do with drugs or, for that matter, with Chris Vogel. Why would she possibly have been put into witness protection? Even if she saw something incriminating the night of the reunion, her entry into the program could never have proceeded that rapidly.

Governments can leak like a sieve, but the witness protection program is famously successful at secrecy. It has to be; if anyone in the program was found and killed, nobody would ever again be willing to enter. It's an invaluable tool that the Feds use to get people to testify against bad guys; they couldn't risk blowing its credibility.

But would they let the police conduct a yearlong investigation looking for two people that were taken into the program? Would they let Vogel's mother agonize all these years, not knowing whether her son was alive or dead? Would Vogel himself let that happen? Those are questions I can't answer, except to say that I don't believe the two are in the program.

I think they're dead.

Laurie and Andy have a friend named Cindy Spodek, who is the number two person in the Boston Bureau of the FBI. Laurie is going to discuss the situation with Cindy and see what she can find out. It's not likely to be much, but it's worth a try.

I finally head home after midnight, and Dani is waiting up for me. "How was your day, honey?" She knows that my day is usually different from that which most people experience.

"Fine. We barged into the office of a bookie who works for an organized crime family and questioned him. In the process Marcus knocked two of his enforcers unconscious; they should be waking up any minute now."

"Ho-hum."

I smile. "Yup. Just another day at the office."

"And, Simon, did you have fun?"

In response, Mr. Tough Dog goes over and licks her face. My partner has something of a split personality.

I have found that Dani, despite her having no experience in law enforcement at all, is a good sounding board when I'm on a case. I tell her about the note that Vogel sent to his mother before he disappeared, and the list of people that were going to the reunion.

"In terms of the list," she says, "I wouldn't read too much into that. People have specific groups of friends in high school, and it sounds like Vogel's group was pretty small. I would want to know my friends were going to be at a reunion before I decided whether to go."

"What about the note?"

"Well, he knew something was going to happen. It certainly argues against a random killing."

It's a good point. "You would have made a good cop."

She laughs. "No chance."

"How about your day, honey?" I know that Dani had a meeting about a large wedding at a New York hotel.

"Much more fascinating than yours. We debated for a half hour whether to serve beef Wellington pass-arounds, in addition to the bacon-wrapped shrimp, chicken skewers, and meatballs."

"I thought Beef Wellington was a wrestler."

"You are a high-society kind of guy."

"So what did you decide? Are you going with the beef Wellington or not? I need to know; don't keep me in suspense."

"No news yet. You don't make decisions that momentous in the spur of the moment."

FRED PRICE WAS QUITE WILLING TO TALK WITH ME.

Once he heard what it was about, he became downright eager. This crime was a big event in Paterson, and talking to an investigator about it probably has a certain element of drama or excitement for some people. I don't understand that attitude, but I've seen it often enough to know it exists.

Fred owns a car wash in Passaic; it's one of those all-automatic places where customers sit in their car while it gets sloshed and sprayed with water and soap. We meet in his office, which thankfully remains dry.

"That your dog?" He eyes Simon warily.

"No, he's getting his car washed and asked if he could join us while he's waiting. I didn't see any harm in it."

Price chuckles uneasily. "Is he friendly?"

"On occasion. Let's talk about the reunion."

"That was some night for me. I reconnected with Michelle

Conyers, who I dated in high school, and we wound up getting married."

"That's nice," I say, though I pretty much couldn't care less.

"But it only lasted two years and we got divorced."

"Less nice."

"Yeah. But then that thing with Kim and Chris, that was wild, huh? I mean, how do you figure that?"

"You sent Vogel a printed list of who was going to be at the reunion."

"I did?"

"Yes. Did he ask for it?"

"He must have; I just don't remember. A lot of people wanted to know who was going, but most of them asked about specific people. A few wanted the whole list, so I probably emailed it to them."

"So you wouldn't have circled a bunch of names on the first page?"

"Not if I emailed it. But I don't remember either way."

"If you emailed it, would you still have the email on your computer?"

He shrugs. "Sure. I don't throw any emails out; I just archive them. Other than spam and stuff."

"Can you look now? I'm interested in emails between Vogel and you."

"Sure. Why not? They would be on my laptop."

He takes out that laptop and starts hitting some keys. After just three or four minutes, he says, "Got it. An email from Chris, and then one from me with an attachment. That was two weeks before the reunion, so it must have been the list. You want to see them?"

"Can you print out copies?"

"No, the laptop is not set up with this printer. I could forward them to you."

"That would be great." I give him my email address and he forwards them. I hear the pinging noise that means I've received them on my phone. I have no understanding of technology, but it's great.

When Simon and I are in the car, I open the emails. The one from Chris says, *Hey, Fred . . . hope you're well. I need a list of who is going to be at the reunion. Can you send it to me? Thanks in advance. Chris.*

The return from Fred simply says, *Here you go . . . it's attached. See you there.*

There's nothing earthshaking here, but one word sticks out . . . *need*. Why would Chris *need* a list? It may mean nothing, but it's a strange way to have phrased it.

Did he *need* to know that Kim Baskin was going to be there?

And while the list that Fred emailed him was seven pages long, Vogel only had the one page, the first one. Is that because Baskin's name was on it? But if Baskin was the only important name on that list, why did he circle around fifty of them?

I don't know that there is anyone still alive who can answer these questions.

IF MONEY IS THE WAY TO KEEP SCORE, THEN HAROLD COLLISON IS PROBABLY number one in our class.

Harold was part of the small group of self-admitted nerdy friends, along with Vogel and Professor Bruce Sharperson, the psychology professor from Rutgers.

But whereas Vogel wound up using up the money he earned selling cars on drugs and gambling, and Sharperson became a college professor (though he must have had a substantial inheritance), Collison hit it big. He graduated from high school nerd to computer nerd and designed software to be used in maintaining medical records, which apparently wound up being used internationally.

If this house in Alpine is any indication, software pays pretty well these days. Collison said he would meet me here, and he comes out when I make it up the long driveway to the front of the house.

It's an enormous place; if they ever decide to move the state capital from Trenton to Alpine, this could serve as the statehouse. It's three stories high, but the elevator I see across the foyer when we walk in means it doesn't quite qualify as a walk-up.

We walk through the house and exit out the back. Two tennis courts and a huge pool are back here; if they put lane markers in, they could hold the Olympic trials in this pool. We sit at a table and a butler type appears out of nowhere, offering me something to drink.

I go for a Diet Coke and Collison takes an iced tea. "Nice place for a starter house."

He laughs. "Yes, I'm hoping to trade up."

We talk for a bit about high school, though it has to be acknowledged that we had very different experiences there, and few common friends. Collison went on to MIT and then Harvard Business School, not exactly a typical route for most Eastside graduates.

We then switch to talking about Chris Vogel, and Collison says, "Chris was the smartest kid in the class; certainly smarter than Bruce or me. He just took a different path."

"Had you kept in touch with him?"

Collison nods. "More than Bruce. Bruce got tired of his attitude; Chris always acted like he was owed something. I tried to help him, but then the drug use started, and I'm afraid I couldn't deal with it. But I still felt sorry for him, and for his mother. She deserved much better."

"Did you know he gambled?"

"No, I don't think so. Or maybe I did; I just can't remember. But I'm certainly not surprised."

"You reconnected at the reunion?"

Collison smiles. "Yes, it was like old times for a few hours, which I suppose is the definition of a reunion."

"Did Vogel act unusually that night? Like he was nervous or anxious? Or that something might be wrong?"

"None of that. He seemed fine, actually in a really good mood. It could be that he was high on drugs of some sort; I'm not very good at detecting that."

"Did you know Kim Baskin?"

"Not well, but we were in some classes together."

Collison says that he's unaware of any relationship between Vogel and Baskin and would be surprised if there was one. "Have there been some new developments in this terrible situation? Why the sudden resurgence of interest?"

"The police never consider a case of this consequence to be closed until there is a resolution."

"Yet you are not the police."

"True enough." There's no reason to tell this guy any more about our role, though I can certainly understand his curiosity.

It's not like he has provided me with a wealth of information. He has absolutely no idea what happened to Vogel and Baskin after they left the reunion that night.

Just like me.

"MR. RUSSO WANTS TO TALK TO YOU."

I hear these ominous words when I pick up the phone. The caller ID had said private caller, and I generally screen those calls. This is one I should probably have screened.

"What about?" It seems like a logical question.

"He'll tell you that when he talks to you."

"So put him on the phone."

"This conversation will take place in person."

Russo probably wants to express his extreme displeasure with our treatment of Anthony Velasco, the bookmaker in Russo's employ. That we left two of Velasco's people out cold on the floor likely didn't help. Velasco's people by definition are Russo's people, and I'm sure Russo prefers his people to remain conscious.

"Where does he want to meet?"

"In an office behind Petrino's Restaurant, tonight at nine P.M."

"No chance."

"'No chance' is not something I would recommend saying to Mr. Russo."

"Really? Then how about 'Kiss my ass, Joseph'? Does that work for you?"

I have a bit of a temper and it comes out when people think they can intimidate me. As a cop, that temper nearly cost me my life a couple of times. On the other hand, it has saved me more times than I can count. Either way, it doesn't matter. It's not something I can control; I came to terms with that a long time ago.

"Is that what you want me to tell him?" He's obviously not relishing saying it.

"I don't care what you say; you can put it into your own words. But he wants to talk to me; I have no particular interest in talking to him. So if Russo wants to meet with me, here's the where and when. Eastside Park, on the bench across from the tennis court, at noon tomorrow."

"I'll give him your message and call you back."

"You don't need to; I'll be there. Just make sure he knows this is a onetime offer."

Click.

I think I offended him, which just breaks my heart. But tough guy as I may think I am, I am not meeting with a pissed-off Joseph Russo in a back-alley office at night. He'd be surrounded by his people, as he always is. Eastside Park in the middle of the day feels a lot safer.

I call Laurie and tell her about the phone call.

"I wonder what he wants."

"Probably to scare me because of what we did to Velasco. If he was going to kill me, he wouldn't call me to a meeting. He'd have someone come up behind me when I wasn't looking and pop me in the head."

"You're probably right. But we're not taking any chances. Marcus and I will be there."

"He wouldn't do anything out in the open in the middle of the day. He's not that stupid."

"Marcus and I will still be there to see to it."

We make our plans, which are not particularly complicated. Basically Marcus and Laurie will shoot anyone who tries to shoot me first. We are quite the strategists.

I head home to pick up Dani and go out to dinner. The first thing she asks me is how my day went, and if there is any progress on the investigation.

This is a tough situation. It's one I've faced before and will undoubtedly face in the future. I could simply say, "Nothing new, honey," which would be an obvious lie, or I could tell her about the meeting with Russo.

The latter approach would worry her. Because of her lack of experience in this area, she would no doubt think that there is some danger in meeting with a vicious head of an organized crime family. Strange, but true.

With most, if not all, of the women that I have dated in the past, lying would have been my default position. It's not like they could be of help, so why tell them?

But Dani's different, in a thousand ways, and this is one of them. Lying to her just seems wrong on a significant level, and I have always tried to avoid doing so. This is what I do for a living, this is who I am, and she needs to know all of it.

So I tell her, and her first question is "Do you think he'll show up?"

"I have no idea."

"I think he will." Before I can ask why she believes that, she asks, "What do you think he wants?"

"Probably to scare me and tell me that if I ever mess with his people again, I'll wind up in the Passaic River with Luca Brasi."

"I don't think so. If that's all he wanted, he could have said it over the phone or sent one of his people to deliver that message. I think he wants something from you, which is why I think he will show up."

I'm impressed by her reasoning, and unimpressed with myself for not having figured it out. "What do you think he wants? You're on a roll."

She shrugs. "How the hell would I know? I'm an event planner. But I'm going to be there."

"Where? In the park?"

"Yes."

"No, you're not."

She smiles. "I don't recall asking for your permission."

"It would be dangerous."

"There will be plenty of people in the park; I'll be one of them. I'm not going to intervene, believe me."

"So why do you want to be there?"

"To see what happens. I worry about you. I love you. And if it goes bad, I want to get my profile on Match.com as soon as possible."

I SHOULD HAVE CHECKED WEATHER.COM BEFORE I SET UP THIS MEETING.

It's been raining since nine o'clock this morning, and the rain has gotten much heavier as noon approaches. It's not a cold rain, but it is definitely a wet one.

This changes things in two ways. First, we're likely to get soaked, whereas I had previously thought we would stay relatively dry. Second, and more important, the park will be empty. Who is going to be hanging out by the tennis courts in the pouring rain?

I pick up Laurie and Marcus at Laurie's house. Since Laurie is the most organized and planful member of the team, she has brought three umbrellas with her. That in itself is amazing; I don't think I've owned three umbrellas in my entire life.

The park is only a few minutes from her house, and we arrive ten minutes before noon. I take one of the umbrellas and go sit on the bench. Laurie and Marcus take up separate positions about twenty-five feet away on each side.

They are out in the open; we want Russo and his people to know that they are there. Marcus doesn't use his umbrella. I think one of his superpowers is that he's impervious to rain.

The only other person I see in the park is Dani, on a bench by herself about sixty feet away. She doesn't wave or react; she just sits under her umbrella and gets ready to find out if she is going to reenter the dating scene.

At three minutes after twelve a black sedan enters the park and pulls up near the tennis courts. Two men get out of the front seat. One of them opens the rear door, and Joseph Russo steps out. The man has a large umbrella, which he holds over Russo as they walk toward me. The second man walks a few steps behind.

Russo sits on the wet bench, takes the umbrella, and holds it over his head. He nods and the two men step back and move away, so that we are now surrounded by a half arc of four people . . . Marcus, Laurie, and Russo's two men.

Something about sitting on a bench in a park, in a driving rainstorm, with the head of an organized crime family, is surreal. At the very least it makes me unique: not many people can have done this.

Russo looks around, sees Marcus, and says, "Clark . . . I should have known. When Velasco told me a guy knocked out his two people in two seconds, I figured it had to be him. What's he to you?"

"He's my partner."

"What kind of partner?"

"We're private investigators."

"What's he doing here?"

"Being a good partner."

Russo frowns. "I should have told my guys to bring bazookas."

"Wouldn't help."

He points to the ground. "What the hell is this green stuff?"

"Grass. You called this meeting?"

"We could have been in my office having a beer. Instead we're sitting in the rain like two assholes."

"Maybe you should get to the point before we drown."

He nods his agreement. "You were asking about Vogel. Why is that?"

"He's missing, along with a young woman."

"Tell me something I don't know. Why are you looking for him now? He's been gone for a hundred years."

"We've been assigned to it by the Paterson PD. They're short manpower." I had already decided to tell Russo about our connection to the cops, on the theory that it might lessen his interest in killing me.

"I had nothing to do with Vogel and the girl disappearing."

Russo's calling Kim Baskin a "girl" irritates the hell out of me, but I opt not to lecture him on political correctness. "You surprised me. I thought you were about to confess."

"Don't be a wiseass," he says, probably good advice.

"So why are we having this meeting?"

"You know who Espinosa is?"

"Of course." Espinosa is a prominent drug dealer in North Jersey, which makes him a rival of Russo's. He's known by the one name, Espinosa, much like Madonna or Cher. The other thing Espinosa is known for is a tendency to be brutally violent.

"He's the one you should be looking at."

"Are you guys not playing nicely with each other?"

"I can eliminate him whenever I want." I am sure this is somewhere between a lie and a drastic exaggeration. "I may be moving in that direction."

"How was he involved with Vogel?"

"Vogel graduated from user to seller, all with Espinosa."

This is the first I've heard of this. "He was dealing for Espinosa?"

"Yeah. He apparently needed the money to pay for his drugs and his losses with Velasco. If you got a kid, you don't want him to grow up to be like Vogel."

"Good parenting advice. Is your point that Espinosa was involved with his disappearance? Why would he want to kill someone that was profitable for him on two levels?"

"Because Vogel was talking to the Feds."

"And Espinosa found out about it?"

Russo frowns at my stupidity. "Vogel disappeared, didn't he?"

Velasco had told us basically the same thing, no doubt because he works for Russo. But I have to admit that the logic is fairly compelling. As motives go, Vogel ratting out Espinosa is a good one.

"How do you know what Vogel was doing?"

"I have access to information."

I take that to mean that he has an informer in Espinosa's operation. "I don't suppose you have anything that would help me prove this?"

"I'm giving you the facts; now it's up to you to prove it." He points to Marcus. "Or you can have Superman deal with it." Russo appears to be suggesting I send Marcus to deal with Espinosa.

"If Espinosa killed Vogel and Baskin, we will bring him down."

Russo frowns, indicating his obvious lack of confidence in me. "Yeah. Just like the Feds did."

With that he stands up, then looks down at the ground. "Grass, huh?" As he starts walking to the car, his two colleagues quickly move alongside him. One of them opens the back door and Russo gets in. The other two get in the front and the car drives away.

The meeting is over.

A good time was had by all.

LAURIE, MARCUS, AND I HEAD OVER TO THE SUBURBAN DINER FOR A QUICK lunch and a discussion about the meeting with Russo.

Dani doesn't join us. When Russo left, she came over to give me a hug and tell me she was glad I was still alive. She then went off to a work meeting, which probably was not about drugs, organized crime, or murder.

Sounds boring to me.

Laurie and Marcus were not close enough to hear what Russo told me, so I repeat it for them. Most of it is not news to us, since Velasco had said much of the same thing. What was new and interesting was the revelation that Vogel was also selling; it places him closer to the inside of Espinosa's operation and makes it more likely that he was actually talking to the DEA.

"Russo clearly has an ulterior motive here," Laurie says. "Espinosa is a rival that he wants to get rid of. But when it comes to saying that Vogel was working with the Feds, he has nothing to gain by lying."

"If Russo knew about it, then so did Espinosa," Marcus says.

I still can't get used to Marcus talking in a manner I can understand. It's jarring every time I hear it.

Laurie mentions that her FBI friend had no information about the possibility of Vogel and Baskin being in the witness protection program, but I say that I haven't considered that a real possibility for a while.

"Why?" Laurie asks.

"I've been thinking about it. Vogel has never testified against Espinosa; as far as I know, the Feds have never even charged him with anything. If Vogel had the goods on Espinosa and he needed protection, why didn't they use him? He wasn't even a witness, so why would he be in witness protection?"

"Maybe even with Vogel they didn't have enough to make a case," Laurie says. "But Espinosa would still want revenge."

"Possible, but unlikely. And Baskin makes no sense at all. Why would she be in the program? I'm not buying it. She gives up her life, her job, her fiancé, because she happened to leave the reunion with Vogel? We have no connection between her and Espinosa, or drugs, at all.

"I think our most likely path right now is through Espinosa. He apparently had a motive against Vogel, and he's certainly violent enough. Baskin might have just been wrong place, wrong time."

"So how do we deal with Espinosa?"

"Russo thinks Marcus should kill him, which is an appealing idea and would clearly benefit society. But it's also murder, which is a bit of a problem. My view is that we should find out exactly what we're dealing with before we blunder into anything. Anybody have a connection at the DEA?"

Laurie nods. "Andy does. He dealt with someone there on a case; they helped each other out. It went well, but I don't think they're big fans of Andy overall."

"That's a surprise." Laurie knows I mean the opposite. As a defense attorney, Andy isn't universally loved by law enforcement. That he can be a pain in the ass exacerbates those relationships considerably. "But I'll bet they take him seriously."

"I'm sure they do," Laurie says. "Let's go talk to him."

We head back to the house. The rain has stopped, and Andy is just coming back from walking their three dogs. Tara, the golden retriever, looks hopefully at me, no doubt thinking her friend Simon may be with me. I feel bad disappointing her.

"I'm assuming the meeting with Russo wasn't rained out?"

"No, went off without a hitch," Laurie says.

"He was as affable as always," I say. "A laugh a minute."

Andy nods. "That's my little Joey."

"We need you for something."

"What am I getting this time? Pizzas? Is lunch on me again?"

"There's a bitter quality to Andy that is somewhat off-putting," I say to Laurie.

She nods. "Tell me about it."

We head inside and update Andy. He has dealt with Russo on a number of occasions and says, "Of course, Russo's only interest in this or anything else is self-interest. His allegiance to the truth is nonexistent, especially if he thinks you guys could be a vehicle to get rid of Espinosa."

"But in this case Espinosa is a viable contender for bad guy in the Vogel and Baskin disappearance, especially if Russo is right about Vogel turning on him and talking to the Feds."

"That he is," Andy says. "I would suggest you talk to the DEA."

"Which brings us to you. Laurie says you have a contact there."

"I worked with them on a case that worked out successfully for both sides. You want me to try and set up a meeting?"

"We do," Laurie says.

"I am again assuming the role of unpaid consultant?"

"You are," she says. "No one could play that role as well as you."

"Can you at least let me in on the secret K Team handshake?"

"Sorry," she says. "That's just for official K Team members. It's an exclusive group. I'm sure you understand."

LILLIAN ASHFORD WAS SEVENTY-NINE YEARS OLD, A MOTHER OF THREE, and a grandmother six times over.

She had lost her husband four years earlier, but fiercely maintained an independent lifestyle. She traveled, read voraciously, and enjoyed a social life with other women in her situation. By all accounts, she was a terrific woman.

At her funeral, eight years ago, the pastor was able to speak knowledgeably about her. He didn't need to learn details of her life from her family so that he could put them into his talk. Lillian had been active in the church, and the pastor had known her for twenty-five years.

So he talked about her loving family, her lifelong friends, her long nursing career, and her volunteer work in the community. It was an overflow crowd, not unexpected for a woman thought of so highly.

After he spoke, Lillian's daughter, Beth, spoke about her

mother so movingly that few dry eyes were left in the room. Neither Beth nor the pastor talked about the circumstances of her death. For one thing, there was no need to, the basics were well-known and publicized in the local media. On this day it was the deadly elephant in the room.

Lillian Ashford was murdered in her home. An intruder entered during the night while she was sleeping and drowned her in the bathtub. The crime had no sexual component, and while the place had the appearance of being ransacked, nothing was missing, so robbery was discounted as a motive.

A motive was never determined, and no suspects were ever identified. But Beth and the pastor didn't get into all of that; it would have been inappropriate and out of place.

One other thing they didn't mention, didn't even know: the police were withholding this specific information in hopes of using it later to confirm guilt should anyone ever come forward and confess to the crime.

Resting above the victim's chest, floating in the water, was a seven of hearts.

ACCORDING TO THE POLICE INVESTIGATION, LUCY DONALDSON WAS THE only person who could be characterized as a girlfriend of Chris Vogel's.

They were no longer together when he disappeared, but the cops thought she was worth interviewing. Who am I to argue?

We agreed to meet at a Starbucks in Fort Lee, which gives me the opportunity to bring Simon without attracting too much attention. People sit outside at Starbucks with their dogs all the time, though few of those dogs are seven-year veterans of the police force.

I grab a table and wait for her to show up. It's a brief wait, as a young woman jogs up the street and comes right over to me. She's wearing running clothes, which is appropriate because she's running.

I had told her I would be with Simon, so she has no trouble picking me out.

"Sorry I'm late."

"You're right on time."

She looks at her watch and smiles. "Then sorry I'm almost late."

I ask her what she wants, fearing she's going to ask for one of those ridiculous Starbucks drinks. I don't want to have to utter words like *nonfat, double-fizz, vanilla, double-shot latte,* so I'm relieved when all she wants is a black coffee and a croissant.

I leave Simon with her and go in and get her order, plus a black coffee for me and a plain bagel for Simon. When I come back, she is petting Simon, who is graciously accepting it.

She seems to want to make small talk for a while, which is generally not my favorite thing to do. But she has a pleasant way about her, and a great smile, so I grin and bear it. She's married, teaches kindergarten in Englewood, and has one child of her own, a three-year-old girl. She even shows me a picture of her.

Finally, without me having to steer the conversation, she says, "Going out with Chris seems like a hundred years ago."

"How long did you date?"

"Maybe six months, give or take a month." She smiles. "Though with Chris, a month usually seemed a lot longer than a month."

"What do you mean?"

"Well, you know how everyone says to have a good relationship it takes a lot of work? My husband and I have since learned otherwise. But with Chris it was true."

"Is that why you split up?"

"Yes, mostly. He was too erratic. And he didn't pass the 'Do

I want this man to father my children?' test. But one thing I'll give him: he was smart. One of the brightest people I've ever met. What a waste."

That sentiment seems to be widespread; Harold Collison, who went to MIT and Harvard Business School, said Vogel was the smartest kid in our high school class. Professor Sharperson said something similar.

"You split up about a year before he went missing? Is that right?"

"Yes. What a horrible thing."

"Was he using drugs at that time?"

She nods. "That's one of the things I meant by erratic. He stopped when we started going out; that was a condition I set. But I could tell it had started up again, even though he tried to conceal it."

"Did he ever talk about where he got the drugs?"

"Not to me. He never even admitted to me that he was using."

"What about gambling? Was that a problem also?"

"If it was, I didn't know about it."

"And did he ever mention Kim Baskin?"

"No. At least not that I remember. He definitely did not talk about his high school days very much."

"Is he the type who would have picked up a woman at a party?"

She smiles. "Never. No chance. Not Chris."

"Why do you say that?"

"Because with all his faults and fake bravado, he was one of the shiest people I've ever met. I would be shocked if that happened."

"What if I told you he wasn't murdered, but simply decided to disappear and start a new life?"

She looks stunned. "Is that what happened?"

"I have no reason to think so; I'm just considering all the possibilities. But would it shock you?"

She thinks about it for a few moments before answering. "No, it really wouldn't. I just could never predict what Chris was going to do. Anything is possible."

I FEEL LIKE WE'VE ALREADY MADE GOOD PROGRESS BEYOND WHERE THE police ended up.

That's not to say that we've solved it; we're a long way from that. But we at least have a viable suspect, and one with a real motive to silence Chris Vogel.

But while that is true, I am not yet fully buying into Espinosa as the killer. One of my problems with it is that the bodies were hidden, never to be found. It's not Espinosa's style; he wears his violence and ruthlessness like a badge of honor.

If Vogel and Baskin were killed because Vogel was ratting out Espinosa, he would have wanted his world to know about it. He would have sent an obvious message that such activities would be met with immediate and vicious retribution. He would have sent up a plane to skywrite the news. Leaving open the possibility that Vogel and Baskin ran off on their own would not satisfy Espinosa.

At least that's my view.

A bigger problem, but one that is a bit down the road, is proving anything against Espinosa. The crime was seven years ago, and no forensic evidence ties him to it. There's also a great likelihood that he had it done anyway.

Our only hope would be in getting someone in Espinosa's organization to turn on him and provide evidence of his guilt.

Good luck with that. Espinosa killing someone who turned on him is a rather big disincentive for someone else who might be considering turning on him.

I've driven down this morning with Laurie and Andy to a meeting at the Federal Building in Newark. I left Simon at their house. Dani's working, and this way he'll have the company of Tara, Sebastian, and Hunter.

Laurie and Andy felt that Andy should be here, since it's his contact we're going to meet. Andy has offered to make the introduction and then leave the meeting, but I said he should stay. He's smart and might have something to offer.

Marcus is not with us. We didn't think it necessary for everyone to be here, and Marcus is busy scouting out Espinosa's organization and his schedule and habits. If we eventually have to deal with him somehow, it's best to have all the information we can at our disposal.

We announce our arrival, and within five minutes we're brought into the office of Agent Luis Alvarez. Andy introduces us and then Alvarez introduces Agent Brian Hedges, who will apparently sit in on the meeting. I don't know which of them is higher up, but it doesn't matter to us.

Referring to Andy, Alvarez tells Hedges, "This is the guy I told you I never wanted to talk to again."

"Stop," Andy says, "you're making me blush."

I'm sure Alvarez thinks Andy is a complete pain in the ass; everybody in law enforcement does. So did I when I was a cop.

And in truth the people he annoys are not limited to those in law enforcement.

But Alvarez obviously respects him because this meeting was set up in twenty-four hours. DEA agents don't usually sit around wondering how they are going to fill up their day. Andy told him this was important, and Alvarez must have bought it.

Andy says, "I'm going to turn the meeting over to Corey, but first let me set up where we are. I told Agent Alvarez that you are investigating the disappearance and probable murders of Chris Vogel and Kim Baskin, and that you have reason to believe that Espinosa is responsible.

"Even though we were talking on a phone and I couldn't see him, I believe Agent Alvarez's ears actually perked up when I mentioned Espinosa. Corey?"

"So first of all, we are looking for confirmation of some things we've learned," I say. "Was Chris Vogel dealing for Espinosa and was he acting as an informant for you?"

"So you're here for information?" Alvarez's annoyance is evident. "Who the hell do you think we are, Wikipedia?" His attitude doesn't surprise me; it's the way the game is played.

"Actually, we think you are someone who wants to get Espinosa off the street, one way or the other."

Alvarez thinks for a few moments, as if making a decision in the moment. It's total bullshit; we all know that whatever he is willing to say was decided before we got here and was cleared with his bosses.

Finally he nods. "Your information is accurate. Vogel was selling for Espinosa, and he was working for us."

"Is that why he started selling?"

"No, we recruited him after that. He started selling because he needed the money. He was working for us because he preferred that to jail."

"Were you paying him?"

"No."

"Do you have any knowledge about what happened to Vogel and Baskin?"

"No. None. But I would be surprised if Espinosa was behind it."

That both surprises and displeases me. "Why do you say that?"

"Because after the murder we did an assessment as to whether anyone tipped Espinosa off about Vogel acting as an informant. We are one hundred percent confident it did not come from the few people in our agency who were aware of it. The only way Espinosa could have found out would be if Vogel told people, and that is highly unlikely. He would have known that if the information got out, he'd be a dead man."

"Yet the word is, in fact, out. How did that happen?"

"Why didn't you ask Russo during your meeting in the rain? Very romantic, by the way."

"How did you know about that?"

Alvarez laughs. "We put two and two together; not the hardest thing to do. We have Russo under constant surveillance. Would you like to see a video of your rendezvous?"

"No thanks; the rain made my hair frizzy." Then, "But while Russo may have had a motive for fingering Espinosa, he was still right about Vogel working with you. How did he find out?"

"We don't know. I wish we did. But we're pretty sure the word got out well after the murders."

"Could Vogel be in witness protection?"

"I will deny I said this, but, no, he is not."

I don't think any of us are surprised by this; I'm certainly not. We had pretty much rejected a while back the possibility of Vogel and Baskin being in the program, but this makes it a certainty.

"We're going after Espinosa; what can you tell us about him?" I ask.

"First thing I'll tell you is be careful. Espinosa would be happy to eat his dinner, get up and cut your heart out, and then have his dessert and coffee. He makes Russo look like Mary Poppins."

"Is he cutting in on Russo?"

"Big-time. Espinosa probably now represents about seventy percent of the illegal drug operations in North Jersey; it used to be fifty-fifty. Russo is worried that he's going to expand into other areas like gambling and prostitution. If he does, it will be war, and I'm not sure Russo can win it. But I'd buy a ticket to watch."

Alvarez is speaking freely, which I appreciate. I'm sure he's doing so for his own benefit; he wants us to put Espinosa away. But that's okay; we share that goal.

Laurie speaks for the first time. "Save your money. We're going to put Espinosa away."

WE DROP ANDY OFF AT THE HOUSE, AND I GO WITH LAURIE TO SIT IN ON AN interview she is conducting.

It's with Cynthia Arkin, a woman who was at the reunion and saw Kim Baskin leave that night. She has indicated that she may have something interesting to tell us, so I figure I might as well be there to hear it.

Arkin lives in the Royal Towers apartment building in Hasbrouck Heights. It's right off Route 80, which is an easy fifteen-minute drive to the George Washington Bridge. Her apartment is on the fourth floor, which makes it about halfway up the building.

It's immediately clear that this is going to be a short meeting. Arkin greets us at the door dressed in a nurse's uniform and apologizes that she's in a hurry. "The hospital just called; they're short a person for the four P.M. shift. So we'll have to make this fairly quick. I'm sorry."

We sit down and get right to it. "Were you and Kim Baskin friends?" Laurie asks.

"Sort of. Not close, but we had some good friends in common. We'd been at a lot of parties together, back in high school, and had seen each other a few times since."

"But you saw her leave that night?"

Arkin nods. "I was sitting at the desk near the door. We were giving out bags of souvenir remembrances of the reunion. Nothing valuable, of course.

"I had just gotten there because it was not that late and people hadn't really started leaving yet. I was surprised to see Kim heading for the door with a guy I later found out was Chris Vogel."

"You didn't know him?" I ask.

"No. If I knew him back in the day, I had forgotten about it."

"Did Kim say anything when you saw her on the way out?" Laurie asks.

Arkin nods. "I said something like 'Are you leaving already?' And she said, 'I'll be back in a few. Don't say anything to Linda.'"

"Who is Linda?"

"Linda Stroman. A mutual friend of ours."

"Do you know why she said that?"

"Not really, but it was Linda's birthday that night. I got the impression that they were going to surprise her with something . . . maybe going to get a cake? I really don't know."

"But she didn't say where they were going? Or why she and Vogel were together?"

"Definitely not to me."

"Did you tell all this to the police?" I ask. If they conducted an interview with her, it was not in the documents we received.

"No. I actually was moving and two days later relocated to Seattle. I was getting married. I didn't know what happened for a few weeks, when a friend from back home finally told me."

"But you didn't tell your story then either?"

"I didn't think it was important; I mean, it was clear they left together, and everyone already knew that. I didn't feel like I had anything important to add. But my friend said there was a tip line set up, an eight hundred number, so I called that and left a message about what happened. I didn't hear back from anyone, so I assumed what I had to say wasn't significant.

"I moved back here last year, but I never thought anything more about it, until you called. Did I do something wrong? Could I have helped?"

"You did exactly as you were supposed to do," Laurie says, trying to make her feel better. "And hopefully you're helping now."

On the way back to Laurie's house, we talk about the conversation with Alvarez, the DEA agent.

"I think we should try and find out just how big a player Vogel was in Espinosa's world. I'm still not convinced he could have hurt Espinosa enough to cause him to kill them both."

"Why do you say that?" Laurie asks.

"He was working with the Feds. Killing him would cause a lot of attention; it's not something Espinosa would have done without carefully considering the repercussions."

"Espinosa's reputation is not as the 'carefully considering' type."

"True. But we can at least partially judge Vogel's importance to Espinosa based on how much he made selling."

Laurie nods. "Worth a shot. We can have Sam get his bank records."

"We can also get a subpoena for them."

"We can do both, but Sam's getting them will save us at least a week."

The logic of that is obvious. "Go for it," I say.

DANI AND I TAKE ADVANTAGE OF SOME NICE WEATHER TO HAVE AN OUTSIDE dinner with Simon in Verona.

I'm feeling guilty that I haven't been spending much time with them, even though Dani has been busy with her own work, and Simon is not the complaining type.

It's a relaxing evening; work is barely mentioned. Most of the time we spend discussing who is the best-fielding third baseman of all time. I think it's Nolan Arenado, while Dani goes with Brooks Robinson. She says this despite the fact that Robinson retired from baseball before she was born, limiting her ability to have seen him play. To hear her talk about him, you'd think she had season tickets to Orioles games back when he was in his heyday.

Dani is a baseball purist and as such always seems to think the old-timers were better. I've tried to offer my view that athletes in all sports are much better now, partly because of training regimens, and that someone in Babe Ruth's physical shape wouldn't even be allowed in the clubhouse today. She rejects that argument out of hand.

Dani has pasta pappardelle, and when she finishes, she says, "That was delicious. You know, we could make this at home."

The idea of either of us successfully cooking anything beyond water is ridiculous. "Which one of us could make this at home?"

She smiles. "I meant if we had a private chef."

"Right. That could work."

Throughout the dinner I see a dark sedan across the street and slightly down the block; I can't tell the exact color in the dim light. But one thing I can make out is a man sitting in the driver's seat. The car is turned off, but he just sits there and at least occasionally looks our way.

We pay the check and leave, heading for our car, which is parked down the street from his, but pointing in the same direction. I pull out and go down the street fairly slowly, watching for him to pull out behind me.

He's there.

I don't bother watching him anymore; I know where I'm going, which means I know where he's going. But I do pull into our attached garage, rather than parking on the street, which I usually do. I don't want to leave Dani and Simon, or myself for that matter, out in the open where the mystery man could take a shot at us.

When we get in the house, I look out the window and see that he is parked across the street, lights turned off, with a view of the house. I tell Dani what is going on, and she reacts calmly. "What are you going to do?"

"Go talk to him."

"Don't you think you should have backup?"

Even though she is probably right, I don't want to risk waiting for Laurie or Marcus and maybe have the guy leave. "Believe me, I can handle this."

I put on a light jacket with a pocket large enough to hold my revolver and my hand. I tell Dani to keep the door locked, then I go out the back of the house. I make my way through my neighbors' yards until I am well behind where I saw his car, then work my way back toward him, taking care to stay out of his possible line of sight.

I am going to approach from the passenger side, point my gun at him, and have a nice conversation.

Which I would do, if his car were still there. But it's not.

I go back to the house and call Laurie to tell her what's going on. We both understand that the surveillance on me is likely going to continue, and we make plans to help us find out what is going on and who is following me, while ensuring my safety.

Laurie says that she will call Marcus and include him. When the goal is ensuring safety, Marcus is an outstanding person to include. And the best part of it is that if he says something, I'll be able to understand him.

When I get off the phone, Dani asks me what I think might be going on.

"I honestly have no idea. I would think it might involve Russo, since he's the only person we've really annoyed so far. But I don't see what Russo would have to gain by tailing me."

I go a little further. "It doesn't seem like it could be Espinosa either. He wouldn't have any way of knowing he's on our radar; Russo certainly wouldn't have tipped him off. Unless there is a leak in Russo's organization, which is a real possibility."

"But what would either of them gain by following you? To see where you're going and what you're doing? Your life isn't that interesting."

"Tell me about it."

"My point is that they may be planning to try and hurt you, or worse."

I nod. "In which case I will hurt them, or worse."

"Your total confidence worries me. I'm afraid you won't be careful."

"Confidence and carefulness are not mutually exclusive."

She frowns. "They were tonight. A careful person would have called in backup before going out to see what the guy was doing out there."

She's got a point.

MY GOAL TODAY IS TO MAKE MYSELF AS EASY TO FOLLOW AS POSSIBLE.

I'm also going to behave normally, since our boy would have no way of knowing that I was aware of his presence last night. I'm sure I did nothing to let him know that I saw him.

I'm not watching behind me because I know that Laurie and Marcus are on the case. If I seem to be in any danger, they will intervene. If there was an Olympic intervening team, Marcus would be a gold medalist. And Laurie is no slouch either.

I take Simon to the pet store to buy some toys. He loves that he's allowed in there and always struts around. He's not a big toy fan; he would prefer to chew on a perpetrator's arm. But he also loves regular, nonhuman chewies, so I get him some, along with toys for Tara, Sebastian, and Hunter.

When I get back in the car, Laurie texts me, *We're on him.*

That information in hand, I head for Eastside Park, as per our plan. I park near the tennis courts and head with Simon for the bench I sat on with Russo. I'm starting to have a sentimental attachment to it.

The next text from Laurie: *He's in the park*. When they get the chance, they are going to approach and question him.

Moments later the sedan pulls up about fifty yards from me. I text back, *I see him. He's right here*.

Much to my surprise, the guy gets out of the car and comes walking toward me. I couldn't tell how big he was when he was in the car, but I can now. He's got to be six-three, and probably 230 pounds, none of it fat. I'm not good at guessing ages, but in this case I'd say early- to mid-thirties.

He's not smiling, but his stride and body language show a lack of nervousness and tension. Whatever this guy is doing, he's comfortable doing it.

Simon gives a low growl as he approaches; his ability to judge people is absolutely amazing. "Take it easy, Simon. This is not the time."

I'm sure Laurie and Marcus are in place, ready to move in if necessary, but I also have my hand in my pocket ready to draw my gun. The guy comes all the way over to me and sits at the other end of the bench, the same spot Russo had occupied when we met.

"You've been following me."

"You only know that because I wanted you to."

I laugh a short laugh.

"Don't believe me?" He reaches into his jacket pocket and I pull out my gun, pointing it at him. If he's scared, he hides it well. "Take it easy, Corey. No need for hostility. Yet."

He continues pulling out a small group of what looks like photographs and hands them to me. I look through them; they are photos of me taken at various places over the last few days.

Two of them send a chill up my spine; Dani is in them with

me. She is centered in the photos as if she was the subject. If there is a message here, he is delivering it effectively.

My concern quickly gives way to anger. This guy is pissing me off; it's taking all my willpower not to grind him into the grass that Joseph Russo didn't recognize. But I need to find out where this is going, and kicking his ass won't get me there.

But there is no question that he is right about one thing: I only noticed him last night because he wanted me to. And on all those other occasions he could just as easily have pointed a gun at me as a camera. "What do you want?"

"To give you a message, that's all, and it's fairly simple. Stay out of Mr. Espinosa's business . . . starting right now. If you do so, we'll be okay. If you don't, we won't."

"That's it?"

He smiles for the first time. "That's it."

His smile is making me more angry, if that's possible. "Since you seem to be a terrific messenger boy, can you give Mr. Espinosa a message for me? You might want to write it down; you don't seem that bright."

The smile is gone and he doesn't answer the question, so I continue, "Tell Espinosa that by the time I get finished with him, he'll be in prison and assholes like you won't even take his calls."

The guy stands up. "Corey, you have no idea who you're dealing with, or what you've just done."

"Maybe he won't have to call you. Maybe you'll be his cellmate."

The guy, apparently not intimidated, walks off, without an apparent care in the world.

I remain on the bench, and a couple of minutes later Laurie comes over.

"Where's Marcus?"

"Following him."

"You heard it all?" Sam Willis had placed a wire on me so we could record everything that was said. I'm hoping it worked; if I know Sam, it did.

"Yes. One thing surprised me."

"That he mentioned Espinosa by name? That surprised me as well. This was not his first rodeo; he had to know that we might be recording it."

"It wouldn't be admissible in court; he didn't make enough of an overt threat for it to be a crime. But it seems careless and overconfident."

"Did you get a good photograph of him?"

She nods. "I did, and so did Marcus."

"Good. I think we have to talk to Pete. But I'll meet you at your place in a little while because first I need to talk to Dani."

I DON'T BEAT AROUND THE BUSH OR SUGARCOAT THINGS WHEN I SPEAK with Dani.

We sit in the den and I tell her everything that happened this morning, after which I show her the photos that the guy gave me. She listens to what I have to say, looks at the photos without expression, then asks, "What happens now?"

"For me? I find out who this guy is and then I try to put him and his boss away for a good long time."

"Will you be able to do that?"

"I won't rest until I do. But I think we have a decision to make. You have a decision to make."

"Which is?"

"Whether you want to leave here until it's over. There is a limit to how well I can protect you, and these people are very definitely dangerous."

"We don't know that they would come after me."

"No, we don't. But it's very possible they were making a veiled threat with these pictures. It wasn't even really that subtle."

"On some level it doesn't make sense that they would try and hurt me. They want you to stop going after them; they would have to know that attacking me would do the opposite."

"They may not be as rational as you. I would just as soon not rely on their devotion to logic."

"Let me think about it," she says. "This is not a situation I've been in before . . . or want to be in again."

"Okay. But in the meantime stay alert and cautious. Very alert and very cautious."

"That I can guarantee."

Dani leans in and hugs me, or maybe I lean in and hug her . . . I can't be sure. But it's working for both of us, and it takes a while before we break it off.

I finally leave to pick up Laurie at her house, so we can go see Pete Stanton together. She tells me that Marcus followed the guy from the park to the Hilton hotel in the Meadowlands. Marcus waited there for two hours to see if the guy was coming out, then left. Marcus had no way to know whether the guy was staying there or meeting someone, and Marcus wasn't too concerned about that anyway. We have the guy's photo so will likely soon have his identity.

"Maybe he knew Marcus was following him," I say, as Laurie and I wait at the precinct to be called into Pete's office. "He was a professional, if he managed to fool me. He might have just gone there to throw Marcus off. He could have slipped out a back door or side door."

Laurie shakes her head. "Not Marcus. Marcus could follow you into the shower and you wouldn't know it."

"That's an image I am going to have trouble unseeing." Laurie starts laughing at that, but stops quickly when I say, "I'm worried about Dani."

"So am I. We need to talk about that; come back to the house afterwards. Andy has an idea."

We're brought back to Pete's office. He has that harried look that all cops have; they teach it at the academy.

We chitchat a bit, then Pete asks, "So to what do I owe this visit? Perhaps an update? So far, if I'm not mistaken, the total amount of updates you've provided is . . ." He points in the air a few times, as if he's adding imaginary numbers. "Let's see . . . seven, carry the four . . . zero."

"Then this is your lucky day," I say. "You're about to get a mega-update."

"Let's hear it."

"Chris Vogel owed money, probably twenty grand, to Anthony Velasco, a bookmaker working for Joseph Russo, Jr."

"Interesting, but a long shot to cause a double murder."

"We're just warming up. Vogel was also using drugs supplied by none other than Espinosa, and he graduated to selling drugs for him as well."

"Growing more interesting by the sentence."

"Vogel was also apparently serving as an informant for the Feds against Espinosa," I say.

"We've officially crossed over into fascinating."

We spend the next ten minutes updating him on the rest of our investigation, including that Kim Baskin apparently thought she was just leaving the reunion for a little while.

"Good progress," Pete says when we're done. "I'm impressed."

"We haven't gotten to the best part," Laurie says. "Corey?"

I tell Pete about the guy following me, including an in-depth detailing of what went on in the park today. Laurie plays the tape, which she somehow managed to transfer to her phone, and we show Pete the photos that the guy had taken of me.

"Not sure Espinosa would want his name thrown around like that," Pete says, which both Laurie and I had picked up on. "Do you know who this guy is?"

"That's where you come in," I say, and Laurie shows Pete the photograph she took of the guy, which she has had printed out. "Do you recognize him?"

"No. But let me keep this and see what I can find out. I don't like that Dani is in those pictures."

"Join the club," I say. Then, "There's one more thing we need to talk about, Pete. It will dictate everything we do from here on in."

"What's that?"

"What's the endgame moving forward?" Laurie asks. She and I talked about this on the way over here. We are obligated to follow Pete's lead on this; as our employer, he's calling the shots.

"What do you mean?" He looks at us, clearly puzzled.

"Is it to solve the case officially or nail the people that did it?"

"I'm not getting it. You consultants are difficult to understand."

I cut in. "Okay. Here's a hypothetical. Let's say we decide, all of us, that we are convinced that Espinosa killed Vogel and Baskin or had it done. And by the way, we're not there yet. But if and when we come to that conclusion, is it enough to put him away on another charge? Or do we have to prove that he killed these two people?

"In other words, does it matter if the case stays officially cold and unsolved, as long as the people who did it are brought to justice?"

Pete thinks about it for at least thirty seconds, then says,

"Good question," after which he thinks for another thirty. Finally, "If it's Espinosa, or whoever, while I would like to close the case, it's more important to take them off the streets."

I've always respected Pete, but he just moved up another notch in my estimation. As a cop, he would get huge credit for officially solving the case, but he just served notice that getting justice done is more important.

Pete promises to let us know if he can find out who the guy in the photo we gave him is. "Just be careful," he says. "Espinosa is a son of a bitch."

I'M SURPRISED TO SEE THAT DANI AND SIMON ARE AT LAURIE'S WHEN WE get back.

She and Andy are hanging out in the backyard with the four dogs. It looks so pleasant and serene that it's hard to remember that we just sat in Pete Stanton's office talking about a vicious murderer.

"What are you doing here?" I ask.

She smiles. "Just enjoying the day, chatting with Andy."

"I can be incredibly charming and witty," Andy says. "It's a side to my personality that I've never shown you."

I nod. "That's for sure."

We go inside and Laurie offers everyone coffee or wine. We all opt for coffee; this is not exactly a wild group. Then Laurie surprises me by saying, "Andy, you have the floor."

Andy nods. "Okay, I'll make it short and semisweet. We all know about the situation in the park today, about the photos, and about the fact that Dani, who we in the crime trade refer to as an 'innocent civilian,' was featured prominently in those photos. I think it's fair to say that we are all disturbed by that."

I look over at Dani to see if she's upset by the conversation, but she doesn't seem to be. She's just listening along with the rest of us. I've got the feeling that she knows where Andy is going with this. I certainly don't.

Andy continues, "So even though there may be no real danger, I would submit that we can't take that chance. I propose that we hire Bill Sampson's company to keep an eye on her. Nothing overbearing; just full-time surveillance from a close enough distance until we're positive that the danger has passed."

I know Bill Sampson well. He's an ex–New Jersey state cop who now runs a small private investigative firm. He's thoroughly competent and reliable; he would be a perfect choice for this job.

I'm not sure how to reply to this; the cost of hiring Sampson and his people 24-7 is way beyond what I can afford.

That doesn't seem to matter, as Andy continues, "Just so we're clear, I'm going to pay for it. It's my anniversary present to Laurie."

Laurie smiles. "It's just what I've always wanted."

I don't know where to go with this. Having Bill on the case protecting Dani would be incredibly comforting to me, but I can't have Andy pay for it. It's just too much.

"It's a great offer, Andy. Incredibly kind and generous. But Dani and I will have to discuss it."

"Andy and I have already talked about it, Corey," Dani says. "As long as he's willing to do it, it would make me feel much better, much safer."

"So the ship has sailed on this?"

"It's been out to sea for a while. Andy and I got off the phone a little while ago with Bill Sampson; he seems really nice. And this way you'll be able to go about your business without having to worry about me."

"Well"—I turn to Laurie—"happy anniversary. When is the actual day?"

"In eight months. Andy likes to get ahead of these things."

We decide to have dinner together here so that we can talk about the case. Laurie calls Marcus and invites him over. We let Ricky, Laurie and Andy's twelve-year-old son, decide what we'll eat, and he votes for pizza. Everybody is fine with that. In fact, I think Andy may have put Ricky up to it.

Just before we place the delivery order, Sam Willis calls and says he has information for us, so Laurie tells him to come over as well.

Everybody's hungry so we order eight large pizzas, four for all of us and four for Marcus. When it comes, I go to the door and pay for it.

I'm a big shot.

We don't talk about the case at all, in deference to Ricky's presence. When we're done, he goes off to his room to do his homework, or at least that's what he tells his parents.

Finally Laurie gives Sam the floor to tell us what he's learned.

"So I went through all of Chris Vogel's financial records. It was not too complicated; all he had was a checking account, an investment account, which he almost never used, and three credit cards. When he died, he had thirty-one thousand dollars in his checking account, eleven thousand in the investment account, and credit card debt of seven thousand."

This is already a surprise. He clearly had enough money to pay his gambling debt to Velasco, and if his life was in any danger as a result of not paying, he could have rectified that easily. Velasco was never a promising suspect, and now he's not a suspect at all.

"Where did he get his money?" Laurie asks.

"That's the interesting part. He brought in money from his job at the car dealership; I'm guessing he was averaging about seventy thousand per year. But that's not where his cash on hand came from, at least not most of it. It was wired from a company called Charkin Credit Limited, based in the Cayman Islands."

"What is Charkin Credit? Did they loan him the money?" I ask.

"As far as I can tell, Charkin Credit is a front; it didn't seem to exist other than as a way to pay Vogel and certainly is not around now."

"Espinosa?" Laurie asks the one-word question.

Andy fields it. "I strongly doubt it. A guy like Espinosa runs a cash business, especially when it comes to paying his people. Why go to all the trouble of covering up payments to Vogel in this kind of elaborate manner when he could pay him in cash and there would be no record of it?"

"I agree," I say.

"The money has to have come from somewhere else," Andy says. "But where?"

"I don't know the answer to that."

"And assuming Espinosa was paying him as well, where did that money go?"

"That's an answer I think I do know," I say. "And I'll confirm it tomorrow."

As we're leaving, I pull Andy aside. "Now I owe you big-time twice over." Andy successfully defended me on a trumped-up murder charge, not accepting any money from me for my defense. Now he's stepping up to make sure that Dani is protected.

"You don't owe me anything," he says. "I volunteered. And as you probably have guessed, it was actually Laurie's idea. I fought against it, but she was relentless."

"Bullshit. But it doesn't matter whose idea it was. I still appreciate it."

"Focus on putting Espinosa away," Andy says, in a rare serious moment. "Dani's not the only one I'm worried about."

MY FIRST STOP TODAY IS TO SEE PROFESSOR BRUCE SHARPERSON AGAIN.

I left a message with his assistant at Rutgers, who said that he did not have classes today. Sharperson called me back an hour later to invite me to his house in Matawan, so that's where I'm headed.

I could have done this by phone, but since I have to be down in this area anyway, and since Sharperson said he'd make time for me, I decided to do it in person.

I'm an old-fashioned investigator in that regard; I like to see people's faces and read their body language when I ask questions. Sometimes it can be more revealing than the words they say. I don't expect much out of my meeting with Sharperson, but one never knows.

The house is in what I would call an upper-middle-class neighborhood. It's quite nice and the neighborhood is well-kept. Sharperson's house is at the head of a cul-de-sac, but if he did inherit all that money from his father, he did not spend it on this home.

Maybe his father didn't leave him anything, which would probably be the only thing we have in common. My father was a cop for thirty years, and if he had any money, I would have gotten it. Unfortunately, he didn't.

Inside, the house is what I would expect from a college professor . . . every wall I see is obscured by bookshelves. I glance at some books, but I'm not familiar with any of them . . . not exactly a big surprise.

There is no evidence of a female touch, so if I had to guess, I'd say that Sharperson is unmarried. But I don't ask him because I don't care either way. I am here for information.

"Are you making progress?" he asks, after fulfilling my request of a Diet Coke. "I've been reading the parts of the newspaper I usually avoid in the hopes that I'll see that an arrest has been made."

"Progress, yes. But we're not there yet."

"Okay, since I assume this is not a social visit, how can I help?"

"There's a piece of evidence I neglected to ask you about."

"And that is?"

"The king of clubs. A playing card was found in Vogel's car, protected by plastic. I'm trying to determine if it has anything to do with his disappearance."

The reaction on Sharperson's face is immediate. "Are you serious?"

"I am."

"That is indeed strange."

"How so?"

He leans forward on his desk. "I believe I mentioned that we were not the most popular kids in high school. We were ultrasmart academics, or nerds, depending on your perspective.

Most of the girls in school would have opted for the nerds description and wanted nothing to do with us, unless they needed tutoring."

"Yes, you mentioned some of that."

"And we did things that were considered uncool. Chess club, biology club, philosophy club; those clubs basically existed because of me, Chris, Harold, and a few other students. I would assume they folded up shop after we graduated, but I can't be sure of that.

"So we reacted in different ways to the lack of social acceptance. Guys like Harold Collison and me, we were comfortable with it. We sort of embraced it, in a way. It's who we were; it's who we are today."

"No desire to be the quarterback of the football team? Big man on campus?"

"None. No one understood or believed that, but it was true. For Chris, it was different."

"He wanted to be the quarterback?"

Sharperson shakes his head. "No, I don't think so, or maybe on some level he did. But he wanted people to understand and accept his lack of interest in those things. He thought that people mocked people like us, usually behind our backs but sometimes to our face. And that drove him nuts."

"He verbalized that?"

Sharperson smiles. "All the time. And I mean *all* the time. I'm sure he was right about the mocking that was going on. He knew that the other kids, especially girls, saw what we were doing, and what we weren't doing.

"Chris used to say that they were going to parties while we were going to our club meetings. He was bitter about it, and whereas Harold and I found it sort of funny, Chris became very self-critical and even self-mocking, as if he bought into what he imagined they were saying.

"But here's the point of this long-winded story. Chris referred to himself as the King of Clubs, because while everyone else was out having fun, we spent our social time in these academic clubs."

As revelations go, this one is pretty stunning. "Did he say this often?"

"Very. This was obviously a long time ago, but I still remember it, and I'll bet Harold does as well. He and I would joke with Chris about it, but I don't think he thought it was amusing."

"How many people would he have said this to?"

"Hard to say. Certainly everyone in the clubs would have heard it, though not nearly as often as Harold and me. Maybe twenty?"

"Then that card being left in the car would be quite a coincidence."

"Mr. Douglas, remember we talked about predictive theory, and how everything is predictable?"

"Of course."

"Well, the flip side of that is that nothing is random. There is a cause and effect for everything, if we look hard enough. The idea that someone would randomly have come up with the king of clubs, without knowing anything about this information I've just told you, is simply not credible."

"Thanks for your time, Professor."

I'M NOT SURE THAT I BUY SHARPERSON'S "NOTHING IS RANDOM" THEORY.

But I have a healthy distrust of coincidences, and this is way too big to be one. If Vogel really referred to himself as the King of Clubs, there is no way that the playing card could have just happened to be there.

That's not to say that it is necessarily a clue to his disappearance, and likely death. He could always have kept it there as some kind of bizarre remembrance of an unhappy time, maybe some kind of strange personal motivator.

He might even have been planning to show it to his friends, a nostalgic throwback that they might all laugh at. Maybe he just forgot to bring it in; maybe he planned to do so when he and Baskin returned.

But it sure as hell is suspicious.

Lessening the likelihood that it means anything significant to the case is the presence of Espinosa. He sure as hell wasn't in philosophy club with Vogel and his friends; nor would Espinosa be the type to leave clever little clues behind. It is extremely unlikely that Espinosa had anything to do with the king of clubs being in Vogel's car.

And Espinosa, through the comments of the guy who he sent to follow me and talk to me in the park, almost confessed to the murder of Vogel and Baskin. He knew we were investigating him, though I'm not sure how, and he sent that guy to warn us off. That's reasonably clear and compelling proof of his involvement, even if it isn't court-of-law proof.

Espinosa also had a clear motive to kill Vogel; he was informing on him to the Feds. In Espinosa's world, that is the ultimate crime, and the penalty is always death.

So until we uncover evidence to the contrary, and I don't think we will, in my mind Espinosa is our killer.

I'm going to have time to think more about this and discuss it with Laurie and Marcus, but right now I'm heading to Freehold to again speak with Brenda Crews, my former English teacher and Vogel's mother.

She seemed a bit anxious when I called and said I wanted to come over. It could be because she's afraid to finally hear about what happened to her son. Or it could be related to something else.

This time it's going to be about something else, and she's right to be anxious. I don't like to do it, but I am going to shake her up a little.

She buzzes me up, and when I get to the apartment, the door is open, and she is sitting in her wheelchair waiting for me. "Mr. Douglas, come in."

I say hello and enter. Her first question is "Anything to tell me about Chris?"

"Just one thing; I know what he wrote on the part of the note to you that was torn off."

I see a flash of fear in her eyes and I'm instantly sorry. I'm not here to cause this woman any trouble, or more pain. But I am here to find out the truth.

Her voice is so soft that I can hardly hear it. "How did you find out?"

"That doesn't matter. It was about the money he left for you. The cash."

She nods; her fear has apparently turned to resignation.

"Don't worry. This is not going to cause you any problems. How much was it?"

"Slightly more than twenty thousand dollars. He said it was mine to keep, but that I should not tell anyone about it. I needed that money, Mr. Douglas."

"I understand. Did he say where he got it?"

"No. He was a good boy. I know he had his troubles, and his flaws, but at his core he was good. A mother knows things like that."

I have my doubts, but I don't voice them. "Do you still have the other piece of the note?"

"No." Then, "Honestly, I don't. I was afraid to keep it."

"What is your income now?"

"Just Social Security."

As I look around the apartment, with a modern television and appliances as well as the electric wheelchair, the numbers don't add up. "Tell me the truth, Miss Crews; I'm going to find out anyway. Finding out things is what I do. But I promise you, I have no intention of taking anything away from you."

"Harold Collison."

"What about him?"

"He was Chris's friend. He sends me money; he has been a godsend. He even calls to check in on me once in a while to make sure I'm okay."

Collison had mentioned Chris's mother to me, and he certainly has a lot of money. I'm not surprised that he's helping her,
but I'm impressed. It's a good, caring thing to do.

"Is there anything else about Chris that you haven't told me?"

"No."

"You haven't heard from him?"

She reacts in surprise. "No. I would give anything to. Do you
think he could be alive?"

I'm not going to lie to her. "I'm sorry, but I don't believe so."

She nods sadly. "I don't either. He would never leave me not
knowing. There is nothing worse than not knowing."

"Thank you for telling me the truth, Miss Crews."

"Thank you for understanding."

"Thank you for the B-minus."

On the way home I call Laurie. "I've got a lot to tell you," I
say.

"Same here. But first, we heard from Pete. He wants us in his
office at four o'clock."

THIS TIME PETE IS NOT ALONE.

There are five of us, more than enough to make Pete's office seem crowded. In addition to Laurie, Marcus, Pete, and me, he introduces us to Captain Mark D'Antoni of the New Jersey State Police.

I have a hunch that D'Antoni wasn't just in the neighborhood; he's the reason this meeting was called.

D'Antoni gives us three photographs to pass among us; all of them are obviously Espinosa's guy from the park. Two of them seem to have been taken without his knowledge, while the third is a mug shot.

"His full name is Leonard Zamora, but he is known simply as Z," D'Antoni says. "His parents brought him here from Spain when he was four years old. They were murdered in their home when he was nineteen, a crime that has not been solved.

"No one would be surprised if Z killed them; there were

many reports of discord within the family. But the case was never made. Let's just say that I doubt that he visits their grave every year to leave flowers.

"He has since been a suspect in numerous murders in various US cities, but has only been arrested once, in Chicago. The key witness against him there recanted her testimony, and the prosecutor in the case believed she was intimidated and threatened. But of course he couldn't prove it."

D'Antoni continues, "He is thought to hire himself out to the highest bidder. Sometimes organized crime; in one case a very rich individual who had grown tired of his wife. She was murdered, but neither the husband nor Z was ever charged. I am giving you the opinion of the investigating detective. That was in Atlanta."

As I am listening, the anger that I felt in the park when Z showed me the pictures of Dani is rapidly returning. It's all I can do to stay seated; I want to get up now and go after him . . . and Espinosa. Whether we officially close this case or not, I am going to see to it that this does not end well for those two guys.

"Interestingly, neither the Feds nor any local cops have anything on him for more than five years; no one knows where he was living, what he was doing, or who he was working for. This is the first sighting of him in all that time.

"The file on him says that he is a martial arts expert, an excellent shot, and particularly handy with a knife. In the murder business that is what is known as a triple threat. He is considered extremely dangerous and highly intelligent, not a great combination."

"Any known contact between Z and Espinosa?" Laurie asks.

"No, and frankly their connection doesn't make a huge amount of sense. Espinosa has always handled his business internally. For him to go outside to bring in Z, and to pay him the kind of money that Z would demand, means Espinosa views the situation as very significant. Espinosa is that rare crime boss that often commits the violent acts himself; he takes pleasure in it."

"You heard the audio from the park?" I ask.

D'Antoni nods. "I did, and the tape doesn't lie. Z is clearly working for Espinosa, which means Espinosa has something big going down. My guess is that you guys are proving to be annoying to him at a particularly inconvenient time."

"We have a tendency to do that. Could he be ready to move in on Russo?" I ask.

D'Antoni shrugs. "Possible, but I doubt it. I don't see much upside in that, at least right now. He's getting stronger, the balance of power is shifting, so waiting would seem to be in his interest. But then again, he didn't call in a guy like Z to make drug collections. It's something way beyond that."

Pete says, "This has obviously become more than a cold case murder investigation. It calls for some department resources in addition to you guys." He looks at D'Antoni. "Maybe some state police resources as well."

"Please hold off on that, guys," I say. "Let us deal with it for a while. If you start going full out, Espinosa might back off, and we'll lose a chance to get him."

"And he would lose a chance to get you," Pete says.

"I think we're willing to take that chance." I look over at Laurie, who nods. Then I look at Marcus, who barely moves his head; I might have woken him. But I'll take it as a yes; the next time Marcus gets scared off will be the first.

"Okay," Pete says. "But I want more frequent updates, and I'm going to pull the plug if I have to."

"Fair enough."

I ask Pete if we can use one of the interview rooms to discuss things among ourselves, and he is fine with it. Before we leave,

D'Antoni gives us a folder, which includes a psychological profile that was done on Espinosa. It's probably a beauty.

Once we're alone, I tell Laurie and Marcus about Sharperson's revelations about the King of Clubs. Laurie thinks it is less significant than I do. She chalks it up to some old high school resentments; maybe he carried it around to motivate himself.

I had the same thought, and I have no better explanation; it certainly doesn't fit with our working thesis that Espinosa ordered the killings. And since Espinosa had the motive of silencing Vogel so he couldn't talk to the Feds, and since Z specifically warned me on Espinosa's behalf, we're certainly not about to abandon that thesis.

"One more thing." I tell them about the cash that Brenda Crews was left by her son. I didn't want to mention that in front of Pete; I don't want to expose her to legal jeopardy, though it's unlikely Pete would go in that direction.

"Twenty grand?" Laurie asks. "That seems like the kind of money he would have gotten selling for Espinosa."

"Right." Marcus jars me once again with a simple spoken word.

"Which leaves us with no idea where the wired money came from," I say, though as I'm saying it I can think of one possibility. "Actually, let me check something out."

ONE WAY OR THE OTHER, WE HAVE TO DECIDE HOW TO DEAL WITH ESPINOSA.

Fortunately, the three of us are in agreement. The chance of us getting hard evidence to use in court in order to convict Espinosa of the murder of Chris Vogel and Kim Baskin is slim.

Fortunately, there is no shortage of reasons for Espinosa to be put away; his crimes are certainly not limited to the case we are working on. If we can get him on anything substantial, then in our minds it's almost as good as solving the cold case.

Deciding to get him is the easy part; figuring out how is a bit tougher. We all agree to think about the best approach. It's something the police and the Feds have been unable to do, but we're just arrogant enough to think that we can do what they have not.

Of course, we operate under somewhat less strict rules than they do. And the angrier I get at Z and Espinosa, the more willing I become to bend those rules even further. It's not something I ever expected of myself, and I'm not proud of it.

It just is.

In the meantime, Marcus is going to keep an eye on the Hilton hotel in the Meadowlands. He had followed Z there after the meeting in the park, but we don't know for sure if that's where he's staying.

No one is registered there under the name Zamora, but that is no surprise. It's likely he'd be using a fake ID. But if Marcus can confirm that he's there, it would be a plus to be able to keep an eye on him.

I call Dani to see how she is doing. Bill Sampson and his people are in place watching over her, but I still can't help checking in. I usually make up a fake excuse for calling, but she knows the truth.

In the meantime, I am continuing my work, which basically consists of driving aimlessly all over New Jersey. My current destination is Cyber Solutions, the Paramus office of Harold Collison. Last time I talked to him was at his house in Alpine; this time we're meeting at his place of business.

For a hugely wealthy software entrepreneur, it's a remarkably small operation. I count four people, including Collison and the receptionist. She's the one who brings me back to his office, which is modern. I would like to be his chrome salesman.

"I don't see much software being manufactured here."

"I don't manufacture it." He smiles. "I created it and then it has a life of its own. People buy it from me, and they use it."

"No one is out there creating a better version?"

"Not so far, and not anytime soon. But eventually they will; it's the nature of the beast."

"So what do you do here?"

"Not much having to do with software or computers. Basically I run an investment company with myself as the sole investor. It helps me pass the time." Then, obviously trying to move this meeting along, he says, "Bruce told me about the king of clubs. That is wild."

"Do you remember Vogel describing himself that way in high school?"

"Absolutely. We thought it was funny at the time, but looking back now, it's seems pathetic. He just had such low self-esteem, and he shouldn't have. He was brilliant, but ultimately bitter and self-destructive."

"He was resentful of the way girls treated him? The way they talked about him?"

"That is without question."

"Would Kim Baskin be in that group?"

"I suppose so, but I really couldn't say for sure. I barely knew her, and I certainly don't know anything about any relationship she might have had with Chris."

"Did you ever wire money to him?"

"What a strange question. Of course not; why would I do that?"

"Why do you send money to his mother?"

He looks at me and smiles. "You do get around, don't you?"

"More than I would like."

"Did you know she taught English at Eastside? She got me to love poetry."

"She had the opposite effect on me. I'll bet she never did you a favor by giving you a B-minus."

"You're right about that."

"So the money . . ."

He nods. "I send her money, not a lot, mind you, because she is wheelchairbound and is living on a small, fixed income. And because she is a nice lady, and the mother of a friend of mine who died much too young. I also check in on her occasionally to make sure she's doing well."

"In what form do you give her the money?"

"With some exceptions, I don't technically give her money anymore, though I would if she needed it. I've made a few interest-bearing investments in her name, and she lives off that interest, plus her Social Security. It doesn't make her wealthy, but hopefully increases her comfort."

"But you didn't give money to Chris while he was alive?"

"No. He never asked, but I wouldn't have done so anyway. I would have been too afraid that the money would have gone toward his drug habit."

I have nothing else to ask Collison; I'm glad he's there to help Brenda Crews. As I'm leaving, he shakes his head and says, "King of Clubs . . . amazing."

GREAT MINDS THINK ALIKE.

Marcus, Laurie, and I have independently come up with the same strategy for going after Espinosa. It's aggressive, but dangerous.

They agree with me that there is no way we are going to nail Espinosa for the Vogel and Baskin murders. The trail has gone too cold; no forensics are to be found and no witnesses are coming forward. We don't even have the bodies. The reasons the case went cold still exist today, and the passage of time makes things even more difficult.

Unlike the cops working the case back then, we know who did it. Like them, we are not close to proving anything legally.

The only disagreement we have is about what, if anything, we don't know. Laurie and Marcus think that since Espinosa had the means and the motive to kill Vogel . . . case closed. Whether we can prove it is not the issue, in their minds.

I have the uncomfortable feeling that even though I agree Espinosa is our bad guy, there's a lot we don't know. I want to learn what happened that night, how Baskin was involved, where the bodies are, and why the king of clubs was in that car, protected in plastic.

None of this makes me any less anxious to put Espinosa away for anything we can nail him on. Unfortunately, there is little chance for us to get him for his drug operations. The DEA, with much greater resources and expertise than we have, has been unable to do it. And we know they have tried hard to bring him down; they even had Vogel as an informant. The likelihood of our being able to succeed where they have failed is slim to none.

So the third option, and the one we've all gravitated to, is goading Espinosa into committing a new crime. We want to annoy him and disrupt his operations to the point where he comes after us, personally, as is his style. It seems to be our only chance to bring him down in the short term.

We've assigned Marcus the task of deciding just how we can pull that off. He's in a good position to do so, since he has been looking into Espinosa's operation for a while now.

Marcus has also been keeping an eye on the Hilton hotel, and it appears that Z is, in fact, staying there. One thing that likely means is that North Jersey is not his permanent base of operations; he is most likely here for a specific purpose and period of time.

As far as we know, he has only left the hotel for meals, which he has eaten alone at various restaurants. On two occasions, when he returned to the hotel, Marcus watched the elevator floors when Z got on and determined that his room was on the seventh floor.

Sam Willis then got involved and searched the guest list for that floor. The only person who was staying at the hotel long enough for it to be Z was registered under the name Steven LaRusso. Sam determined that it was a fake identity, which is how we know that Z is staying in room 708, which is a suite.

Sam also placed a GPS device under Z's car, which he says is a rental in the fake ID name, so from now on we should have a good idea where Z is at all times. It's not foolproof; he can obviously go somewhere in a different vehicle or can even discover and remove the device. But we just don't have enough manpower to follow him full-time, so this is the best we can do.

Sam also finds out that Z flew into town from Chicago three weeks ago, again using that fake name. That's illegal, and something we might be able to get him on later, should we need to. But right now we're after Espinosa; Z is just a means to an end.

Z seems to be in a waiting mode, as if something big is going to happen, and he knows he won't be needed until then. One thing is certain: he's not hanging out in the Meadowlands on an extended vacation, going to the racetrack, or waiting for the Giants home opener.

I can feel myself switching my attention from an attempt to solve the murders of Vogel and Baskin to our new goal of bringing Espinosa down. I'm not completely comfortable with it.

I know that similar justice would be done in either outcome, but I also know I won't feel completely good about it unless I know exactly what happened to the two people after they left the reunion.

Furthermore, the king of clubs is still bugging me. I realize that Espinosa couldn't have anything to do with that because it's unlikely that he even knew about the nickname, and it was probably just some conceit of Vogel's that made him carry it around. But I have to wonder what it says about his mindset, even if it doesn't necessarily explain his death.

If he had such low self-esteem and was in major trouble with drugs and gambling, he could have been desperate. Add to this his bitterness at the way girls viewed him, and it would make sense to consider the possibility of a murder-suicide.

If he had a self-loathing, coupled with an anger against the women in his life, his killing himself and one of those women seems an idea worth considering. Possibly something happened at the reunion that set him off. Maybe Baskin laughed at him over something.

Arguing persuasively against the possibility of a murder-suicide are the circumstances themselves. His car was found at the rest stop; how would they have left there? And how do you hide your own body, to say nothing of your victim, after you commit suicide?

One way would be to do it out on the ocean, drowning both of you. But there is no evidence that he would have been able to get himself and Baskin to open water, and no such boat was ever found.

Hovering over all of this is Espinosa. His clear culpability makes all of this other stuff just idle speculation.

But finding out the exact circumstances of Vogel's and Baskin's deaths, and maybe the location of their bodies, would be an unexpected bonus.

The real target right now has to be Espinosa.

EDDIE GLOVER COULD BEST BE DESCRIBED AS A MIDDLE-LEVEL EXECUTIVE.
In a normal corporation, his title might be manager or director or even vice president, depending on the structure of the company. But Eddie works for Espinosa, a somewhat unconventional employer, so titles aren't given. One's stature in the company is understood by the only person who matters . . . Espinosa.

Eddie is one of five people with the same job responsibilities. He is in charge of dispensing drugs to a lengthy client list, and collecting money in return. There is nothing complicated about the process; everyone is a willing participant, the prices are set, and the mechanics of it rarely change.

Marcus Clark has been watching Eddie and preparing for an interaction with him, a disruption in his normal course of business. Eddie is not aware of this and won't be until Marcus wants him to be.

Then it will be too late.

Marcus would have made a great general, or tactical commander. I've worked with SWAT teams, and he approaches things in the same way. As fearless as he is, he still anticipates every potential problem and structures an operation so as to minimize risk and maximize the chance of success.

SWAT teams bring enough firepower to quickly dominate a situation and overwhelm the target. Marcus brings Marcus.

Marcus has updated us on the planning for the Eddie Glover operation. It's not very different from the way we dealt with Anthony Velasco. That's because their base of operations is similar, which is not a surprise.

Executives in these types of businesses generally don't have their offices on top of corporate high-rises, or in castles surrounded by moats. They need to be on the streets, where their business is, where their customers are. Which makes them easy to find, but tricky to deal with.

Espinosa has his "executives" spread out geographically based on the areas they cover. Glover's domain is downtown Paterson, and he operates out of an office behind a bar on Market Street, not too far from Eastside High School.

We met with Marcus this afternoon to go over the plans. Complicating matters a bit is the outer office between Glover's office and the alley. Entering that way would be dangerous, giving Glover and his bodyguards more time to react. By the time we got to Glover's office, we could be greeted by more than just smiling *Hellos*.

According to Marcus, Glover has three men with him at all times when he is at the office. Customers come to them, to pick up merchandise and pay their money. Therefore, something valuable is always on-site, either the drugs or the cash . . . usually both.

The evening's activities generally end between ten forty-five and eleven. Then the group of four takes what is now mostly money and brings it to Espinosa's main office in Haledon. Espinosa is usually there himself, but that doesn't matter to us right now. We're focused on Glover and the Paterson location.

Glover travels in a van, and it is always parked down the alley, about fifty feet from the entrance to the office. We need to make our move between the time they leave the office and reach the van. That's when they will be most vulnerable.

Marcus tells us exactly where we need to be and when we need to be there. An empty office not far from the car will serve as our base of operations and our "interrogation room." Marcus has picked the lock, so Laurie will be waiting in there for us to bring Glover and his men to her.

We get in position at ten fifteen and settle in for a fairly long wait. Fortunately, it turns out to be an early night, and we see them leave the office at ten thirty-five. As Marcus predicted, one of the men has his gun drawn, and he walks a step in front of the others. Glover is in the center, holding a bag, which obviously contains the evening's cash haul.

Marcus is up against a building, shielded by a Dumpster. Simon and I are behind a parked car, across the alley. It's dark, which certainly helps a lot.

When they reach the designated spot, I whisper, "Gun!"

Simon literally leaps into action. He jumps out and latches on to the arm of the gunman, who drops the gun to the ground in pain and surprise.

Something about a snarling animal in a surprise attack is far more frightening and intimidating than if I had just yelled, "Freeze!" In that case, the man might have turned and fired; in this instance he never had a chance to do so. He was too shocked and scared.

I follow Simon out and get my chance to yell, "Freeze, assholes!" I throw in the expletive because it alerts them to the fact that I do not regard them as significant adversaries. It also demonstrates that I view them with disdain. For instance, it's a lot more effective than "Freeze, colleagues!"

Since I'm holding a gun in my hand, they just stand there, stunned. I tell Simon to let go of the guy's arm and he does so; Simon must have gotten a good piece of it because the guy continues moaning in pain. It's a heartbreaking moment; I don't think there's a dry eye in the alley.

Marcus appears from the other side. He's not holding a gun; he doesn't need to.

Laurie opens the office door and I order them to go inside. Three of them move in that direction, while one of them hesitates. Marcus grabs him by the collar and tosses him against the Dumpster. Unfortunately for the guy, it's not a rubber Dumpster, but rather a metal one. His scream of pain pierces the otherwise quiet alley. When he bounces off, Marcus pushes him into the office with the others.

We line them against the wall, and Marcus frisks them. The guy on the left, the largest and obviously the dumbest of the group, tries to push Marcus and reach for his gun before Marcus can get it. That prompts a short Marcus left hook, which puts an end to the guy's consciousness for the rest of this get-together. Marcus then reaches down to the prone body and takes the gun.

It's dark in here, but Laurie and I have flashlights, which we shine in their faces. The bright glare makes them wince and increases the intimidation.

Glover is the second from the right, and he is still carrying the bag. Laurie walks over to him. "I'll take that." When she reaches for it, he hangs on to it, until I walk a step toward him with the gun and say, "You have a hearing problem? She said she'll take that."

He finally gives it to her. Glover summons the guts to

say, "You know whose that is? You know who you're messing with?"

"You mean Espinosa?" I ask. "You tell that little punk that Corey Douglas said this is just the beginning."

"He'll chew you up," Glover says.

"He better be tougher than you." I shine the flashlight on the bag of money in Laurie's hand. "Thanks for collecting this for us."

"Espinosa will get it back."

I smile. "That will give us something to look forward to."

Before we leave, we handcuff them to two radiators in the room and laugh at them as we leave. We could have just taken the money from them in the alley, but we wanted a chance to talk to them and humiliate them in a way designed to infuriate Espinosa.

Unless Espinosa's reputation is 180 degrees off, this should do the trick.

ALL WE CAN DO NOW, AS FAR AS ESPINOSA IS CONCERNED, IS PLAY DEFENSE.

If his reputation is anywhere near accurate, he'll come at us, most likely me. It may take more goading to get him to do it personally; he might even send Z to do the job. Because of the GPS on his car, we'll have a good idea when Z is coming.

But either way, we'll be ready. Marcus is going to be our lookout, watching over me and ready to alert me and move in if there is any trouble. He also knows the location that Espinosa works out of, but we think it makes more sense to use our personnel around me, rather than keep track of him.

Bill Sampson has added one of his men to my guard, without having to lessen the protection around Dani. Also, Andy's partner in his dog rescue operation, Willie Miller, has offered his services, and we've accepted as needed. Willie can handle himself very, very well. All in all it's an unusual group that could be described as ragtag, but effective . . . hopefully.

So if and when Espinosa comes for me, we'll know it. In what can only be described as a real character flaw of mine, I'm looking forward to it.

Pete Stanton unofficially knows what is going on and is prepared to send officers to any scene that we call him to. We're as ready as we can be.

In the meantime, we have the money that we took from Glover. It's a little over $9,000. We decide to hold on to it for now and then either give it to the police or maybe a charity. We can decide that later.

Technically, we committed an armed robbery in that alley. It certainly fits the definition; we were armed and we robbed Glover of the money. It's not exactly something I envisioned myself doing when I was in the Police Academy, but I'm strangely not regretful about it.

It was drug money, illegally obtained. I have no doubt about that, but if I'm wrong, if Glover or Espinosa earned the money by running a newspaper route or selling lemonade, then they should be down at the police station now filing a complaint. Somehow I don't think that's going to happen.

More irritating to me is that the police or the Feds don't regularly do what we just did. Marcus had no trouble at all getting enough information about Espinosa's operation to enable us to invade his turf. The police could do the same thing if they'd make the effort.

The problem is that they want to deal with the big picture; they want to bring Espinosa down. It's a noble goal, but maybe not the best way to go about it.

They don't think in terms of attacking him at the edges, yet it could ultimately prove effective. We did so because we want to piss Espinosa off, to have him come at us, at me, but the cops could do this maneuver to good effect.

But our doing so clearly invites danger, so unfortunately it's time to have a tough conversation with Dani, and I head home to do that.

Much to my surprise, Bill Sampson is with her in the kitchen. He's eating what would look like scrambled eggs if scrambled eggs were made out of pale bricks.

"This is fantastic," Bill says. "Does she make these for you all the time?"

Dani shrugs and holds her palms up, outstretched, as if to say, *I don't get it either.*

"Not all the time," I say. "But Dani's quite the cook. I can't remember the last time she made something for me that I didn't like."

Once we're finished marveling over Dani's cooking skills, I say, "I think you should move back to your place for a while."

"We've been through this," she says. "I feel safe with Bill and his people watching out for me."

"I know you do, but we're taking it to a new level." I've kept her up-to-date on what is going on, but I still want to be clear about this. "The potential for violence has increased substantially, and it could well be imminent."

"You think he'll come after me?"

"I don't think so. He'll come after me; we're actually trying to provoke him to come after me. But if you're here with me, you will be in danger, and the truth is, it will be harder for me to react."

"Because you'll be worried about me."

"Right. And it will also be easier for Bill to protect you in your house. The way your neighborhood is set up, he would be better able to see someone coming. I don't think that will happen, but I'd feel better knowing he can do the job. Bill?"

He nods and speaks with his mouth still full of egg. "It would be easier at your place, but we'll do what is necessary here or there."

"I don't want to leave."

I nod. "I know that, and I really don't want you to. And it's your decision to make, one we can revisit as we go along. But I don't think this is going to take long to come to a conclusion, so I think it's the smart way to handle it."

She thinks for a few moments. "Okay. We'll try it for a while, but I can't promise for how long."

"Fair enough."

Finally finished with his eggs, Bill says, "I'll give you guys some privacy to wrap this up." With that, he leaves.

Dani says, "Just one thing. I understand you feel a need to protect me, but you have an annoying habit of not protecting yourself. You can't take chances with this; you can't be a hero."

"I hear you, but keep in mind that I have experience I can draw on."

"You have experience in pissing off a vicious drug dealer to get him to try and kill you?"

I smile. "Well, maybe not that specifically. Look, I know I haven't always been as careful in the past as I should be, but things have changed."

She appears skeptical. "What's changed?"

"You."

I'm relieved that Dani is moving out for the time being. Obviously I'll miss her, but not having to worry about her is a big load off my mind.

For now, while we wait for Espinosa to make a move, we also need to get back to investigating the case we were hired to solve, the murders of Chris Vogel and Kim Baskin.

It's not that we consider it a whodunit . . . we feel quite confident that Espinosa "dunit." He had the motive: Vogel was an informant within his ranks. And Espinosa certainly tends toward violence; that has long been established and is about to be demonstrated again.

But if we keep looking at the case, there's a long-shot possibility that we will actually be able to nail Espinosa for it and put it in Pete's "officially solved" file. That would be nice indeed, and it remains a significant part of my goal.

Parts of this case still represent a departure from what I would typically expect of Espinosa. Informants are an occupational hazard for someone like him; they pose an existential threat to his operation.

Without question he would do anything he could to prevent future employees from turning on him. There could be no greater deterrent than demonstrating that doing so would absolutely result in revenge, in violent death.

Why would he therefore just make Vogel disappear? Espinosa would be more likely to hang Vogel's head from a tree in front of City Hall. The way it was done left a great deal of doubt; some people still believe that Vogel and Baskin took off to start a new life. It would have been in Espinosa's interest to make everyone in his world know exactly what happened.

Baskin's disappearance is also strange, at least as it relates to Espinosa. He could have taken Vogel whenever he wanted; why do it when a witness was present who would have to become another victim? She represented an unnecessary complication, and one that would draw even more publicity to the case.

I'm also still troubled by how it came about that Vogel and Baskin left the reunion together. There is no evidence that they had a relationship; where were they going and why did she think they were coming right back?

Was she an innocent bystander, or a key player?

Beats the hell out of me.

I'M NOT SURE WHY I KEEP FORGETTING TO DO THINGS.

I had initially forgotten to ask Professor Sharperson about the king of clubs, and now I've realized I should have asked Cynthia Arkin something when I talked to her the first time. They're not big things, but it shows sloppiness on my part. Sloppy is not a sought-after attribute in my business.

So I'm back in Hasbrouck Heights talking to Arkin, who was the cochairwoman of the reunion committee. She was the one sitting at the desk near the door when Vogel and Baskin left, and Baskin told her she would be back soon.

"You said that the reason you were near the exit was that you were giving out gift bags for people to take."

"Right. Some cool little things that would only have meaning for our class. Also photographs that we took of them coming in. People really liked it."

"And they got these bags as they were leaving?"

"Yes."

"Did they sign anything showing that they got the bags? So that you could cross their names off a list?"

"I think so. Yes, I'm sure of it."

"Do you have that list?"

"I'm sure I must. I have everything from the reunion in storage because we're planning another one in three years. The big twenty-five; I hope you'll be there."

"Wouldn't miss it for the world," I lie. "Could I see the list?"

"I can get it out of storage for you. Mind if I ask why you want it?"

"I can't really say much about it, but I'm trying to determine if anyone might have gone out a different door, and who those people might be."

What I don't say is that if they did, they could have been at Vogel's car, waiting for them when they came out. It's a major long shot, but the results could conceivably be interesting.

"Okay, I'll get it out today. You might also want to look at the poster."

"What poster is that?"

"We had a big reunion poster. . . . It was a photograph of Eastside, and people signed it as they left. I could probably go through it and see who didn't sign. If I recall, pretty much everybody who went out either got the bag, signed the poster, or usually both."

"I know it's a lot of work, but if you could look at both things and compare it to the attendees, that would be very helpful."

"Glad to do it."

I give her my number to let me know. This was probably a waste of time, but it gave me something to do while waiting for Espinosa to kill me.

When I get home, I take out the documents from the original

investigation of the murders. I'm still particularly interested in the king of clubs. Professor Sharperson told me that a limited number of people would know that Vogel referred to himself derisively that way in high school.

If I could get the list of the people who were in the same clubs as Vogel, since they would be the ones who would have heard him say it, I could compare that to any lists that Cynthia Arkin might come up with.

It's the investigative version of grasping at straws, though in this case it's grasping at cards.

As I'm reading, one thing strikes me that I hadn't noticed before. I had seen that the officers had run the king-of-clubs clue through the NCIC database. If a similar clue was part of another crime anywhere else in the country, it would show up and be kicked back to the Paterson cops. That did not happen in this case; nothing was kicked back.

But this database does not reward specificity. The more general the clue, the more likely it is to turn something up. What it turns up may then be meaningless, but that's for the investigator to determine.

In this case, Sergeant Michael Morano submitted the information to NCIC. As it relates to the card, he submitted the *King of Clubs* and got nothing in return. He accepted that and moved on; I'm not going to.

I call Sergeant Katy Seiffert, who is in charge of the department at Paterson PD that deals with these things. Fortunately, I know Katy from my time on the force, and we've always gotten along well.

We spend three or four minutes updating each other on our lives, then I tell her that we're working on this case. I tell her that she can confirm this with Pete, but she says that won't be necessary.

I direct her to the specifics of what I want, and she pulls it up on her computer, which takes a couple of minutes because the case is so old. "Morano submitted the *King of Clubs* as the clue," I say.

"I see that. What about it?"

"I'd like to try it again, but less specific. Can we just say *single playing card*? Or just *playing card*?"

"We could do both."

"That would be great."

Our business over, she seems inclined to reminisce, but I get off the phone because I have a call coming in from Sam Willis.

"Your friend Z was down at Espinosa's office for about an hour."

"You sure?"

"Well, I'm sure his car was there. The GPS doesn't lie. He parked nearby, then left and went back to the hotel."

I thank Sam and get off the phone. I should probably be encouraged by this news; maybe this means that things are happening. But it's not exactly shocking; Espinosa had sent Z to warn me off, so Z obviously works for him. That they might meet is to be expected. I call Laurie and Marcus and update them.

I've successfully filled up most of today with probably meaningless investigative efforts, just waiting for Espinosa.

THIS IS DAY TWO ON THE ESPINOSA WAIT.

It's already getting on my nerves, which may be part of his plan. Maybe he thinks I'll get anxious and fearful enough that when he finally makes his move, I'll just surrender or commit suicide.

He has got to be stewing over our taking his money from Glover. I'm surprised he didn't respond immediately; his reputation is not one of restraint and thoughtful strategizing. I wonder if Glover came up with some way to conceal what happened; he could have feared Espinosa's wrath at his letting us take the cash from him.

I was lying in bed last night, alternating my thinking between wondering when Espinosa would come at me and wondering when I wouldn't have to sleep alone anymore, when it hit me. If I'm trying to predict what Espinosa will do, why not consult an expert in predictive theory?

I called Professor Sharperson first thing and told him I wanted to put his theory to the test. He laughed and said that I should come right down to his campus office, that his first class today is not until two o'clock.

"I see you more than some of my students," he says when I enter his office.

"You should be flattered."

"When Chris first went missing, the police only spoke to me once. This is your third time; I hope that means you're making progress."

"Less than I'd like, and this isn't really about Chris."

"Then I'm intrigued."

I ask him if he will treat what I am about to tell him in confidence, and he says that he will. I go on to tell him about Espinosa, and without getting into specifics, I say that I have done something that is bound to infuriate him.

"I didn't come empty-handed. I've brought you some reading material." I hand him the psychological profile that the police had done on Espinosa. It's about ten pages, and it takes him twenty minutes to go through it. He doesn't say a word, just stays totally focused on what he's reading. Maybe that's why he's a professor and I'm not.

He finally finishes and looks up. "An interesting character. I'm not sure antagonizing him is an approach I would employ."

I smile. "It is unconventional at best."

"So tell me why I just read this?"

"Your specialty is predictive theory. I'm hoping you can predict what he is going to do."

"The fact that I am a supposed expert in predictive theory, and that I understand that human behavior is never random, does not make me a fortune-teller."

"But it makes you smarter than me."

He laughs. "Since you've deliberately made this person an enemy, it's obvious that I'm smarter than you."

"So what is he going to do?"

Sharperson thinks for a few moments. "I'll tell you what I think, but not as an application of predictive theory; rather I am drawing on my experience as a psychologist. Please do not take it as anything more than informed speculation. I do not want to feel a responsibility for your demise, should that be the result."

"That's a deal. My demise is my own responsibility."

He nods. "Okay. Any one of my students could tell you that he is not going to accept humiliation. It would go against every word in this report; my guess is he would be psychologically incapable of inaction. Forgive the double negative."

"I didn't notice it. Will he come himself?"

"My view would be no, at least not initially. As impulsive and violent as he is, he is also street-smart. He has survived, apparently thrived, in a brutally dangerous world that requires innate intelligence. I assume he has violent people at his disposal that he can employ?"

"A large supply."

"Then I would expect he would utilize them as a first step. If they succeed, he will get ample satisfaction. If they fail, it could enrage him to the point where he would need to handle things more personally."

"You think it will be soon?"

"If you'll excuse a very old and bad joke, if I were you, I wouldn't buy any green bananas."

IT'S NO SURPRISE THAT SIMON HEARS IT BEFORE I DO.

I hear his low growl and I'm instantly awake; I haven't exactly been sleeping soundly. I look at the clock and it's one thirty, a logical time for someone to make their move.

I've also been sleeping in my clothes in a guest bedroom. Unlike my bedroom, it overlooks my driveway. The only way that someone could throw something through the window would be to enter that driveway, and there is no possibility that Simon wouldn't be on to them before they managed it.

"Take it easy, buddy," I say softly. "It's under control."

But his head perks up again, facing toward the rear of the house. There is no doubt that something is going on.

"Simon, my boy. I think it's showtime."

I slowly open the bedroom door, standing to the side and keeping Simon there as well, just in case someone is waiting on the other side to fire at me.

I still haven't heard anything, which is a sign that whoever is out there in my protective detail hasn't engaged with the intruders. If they had done so successfully, I would think I would know about it already. None of this reasoning comforts me.

Simon and I wait at the top of the stairs. If anyone is able to penetrate the house, the only way to get to us would be this stairway. If we have the high ground, waiting to pick off whoever approaches, we should be in good shape.

I still can't hear anything, though based on Simon's reaction, he can hear plenty. I keep him calm and in place; the last thing I want to do is alert our assailants that we know they are out there.

The first sound I hear is not faint; it's a crashing noise that sounds like the house is coming down. Then I hear another, similar one. It's like an earthquake, and then an aftershock.

I don't have the slightest idea what is going on, but my phone rings, so I am about to find out.

"Hello?"

"Open the door." It's Marcus's voice, which is a good sign.

Although it borders on inconceivable, I have to be cautious and take into account that someone could have forced Marcus to make the call. As ludicrous as that is, I keep my gun ready when I go downstairs and open the front door.

A heaping pile of humans is lying in front of the door. It looks like two people. One of them is large; it's hard to tell how big the other one is because the large one is lying on top of him.

Putting two and two together, I deduce that Marcus had thrown them against the front door, one at a time. Maybe he was using them as a battering ram to knock it down, but it's more likely that the door was the nearest hard surface for him to toss them against.

Marcus doesn't say anything; he just drags them in one at a time and dumps them in the foyer. He drags the first one by an arm and the second by his collar. I'm about to close the door be-hind them when I hear a different voice: "Leave it open."

Willie Miller is approaching, dragging a third unconscious guy by his collar. The guy is also big, but Willie doesn't seem to be having any trouble moving him.

"How's it going?" Willie asks nonchalantly, as if we are just seeing each other at the movies.

"Okay, nothing much going on," I say, as he drops the third guy near the other two. "Is that all of them?"

"Yup. I'll be right back."

Willie goes outside and comes back with three handguns, which I assume belong to the three guys on the floor. He puts them on the table in the den. "Man, I haven't had this much fun in a long time. Thanks for including me."

I debate whether to call Laurie, but decide there's no reason to wake her. I send her an email and text telling her to call me when she wakes up.

Then I call Pete Stanton and wake him up. He doesn't seem to mind, but he must be starting to regret hiring us by now.

"Everybody okay?" he asks, after I explain what happened.

"Except for the guys who tried to break in."

"That's what I like to hear. See you in a few."

As I'm waiting for the cops to arrive, I'm thinking that Pro-fessor Sharperson was right; Espinosa's first try would be to send people. Chalk one up for predictive theory.

But a second try is coming.

PETE STANTON ARRIVES ABOUT FIFTEEN MINUTES AFTER THE PHONE CALL, and by then eight other cops are on the scene.

One of them is Lieutenant Gary Lansing, who will be the lead detective on the case. Pete is in charge of homicide, and this isn't one, although it was intended to be. Pete had alerted Lansing as to what the situation was, so little explanation was necessary.

By the time Pete arrives, two of the three intruders have regained consciousness, though they are not fully coherent. Apparently my door is really solid, although it's possible that they were already out cold before Marcus used them as javelins.

I have no idea what Willie did to knock out the third guy, but he hasn't come to yet. I think I see a flash of pride on Willie's face that his guy was out colder than either of Marcus's. Competition is beautiful.

The two conscious guys are placed under arrest and have already made it clear that they won't be talking. They are far more afraid of Espinosa than they are of the police, which is a logical position for them. The third will be arrested as soon as he is able to hear a Miranda warning.

In the meantime, medics are on the scene, and all of them will be taken to the hospital with concussion symptoms. Marcus has long been a leading cause of concussion symptoms, and Willie may not be far behind.

Marcus, Willie, and I all have to sign statements, which takes almost two hours. Simon is exempt, so I give him a chewie and he goes off to the corner to chew and watch. Before long he is asleep, which I envy.

When the cops and medics finally leave, I thank Willie and Marcus and tell them they can go home, that there won't be another attempt tonight. They nod their agreement, but I have my doubts that they will actually listen to me. Probably not.

Obviously it's good that we were able to easily ward off this first effort by Espinosa, but there's a negative side to it as well. Espinosa will now have an idea of what we are doing, and how we are defending against him.

Next time he will come at me in a less conventional manner, and with more firepower. As Sharperson said, he is street-smart and a survivor.

The adrenaline having worn off, I sleep soundly for the next four hours. Laurie wakes me up with a phone call at eight o'clock. "Sounds like you had a fun evening. Sorry I wasn't there for it."

"It's a shame you missed it; we had quite a turnout. Anybody who's anybody was here."

"You okay?"

"I'm fine; I didn't do anything. Marcus and Willie handled everything."

"Next time Espinosa will come harder," she says.

"I'm aware."

"Maybe we shouldn't sit around and wait for him to make a move. Maybe we should go on offense."

"What do you have in mind?"

"Sam has come up with something that we might be able to use. Come over later and we'll talk about it. Sam will be here in an hour."

"Will do. The idea of going on offense is very appealing to me."

Next I call Dani to fill her in on the evening's activity; she's a part of this and has a right to know what is going on.

"Can I assume this doesn't put an end to it?"

"I'm afraid not, but we're in the homestretch."

"When this is over, we owe Marcus and Willie a meal. Maybe I'll make them eggs."

I laugh. "I was hoping you'd make some for Espinosa."

I shower and dress and am about to leave for Laurie's when Cynthia Arkin calls. "I've got some information for you."

"That was fast."

She laughs. "My life is not exactly bursting with activity. Anyway, I opened the reunion bin; it's in one of those public storage places. The bad news is that the poster won't be of any help; a lot of people signed it, but quite a few of the signatures are impossible to read. As we get older . . ."

"Believe me, I know."

"But I have the list, and amazingly we also kept the bags that were never picked up at the door. There were names on each, so I know exactly who didn't pick up their bags. I also didn't see their signatures on the poster, but as I said, it's impossible to be sure."

"Who are the people?"

"Jeannie Wallace, Adam Renteria, and Julie Packard."

"Do you know them?"

"I know Adam and Julie really well; we still get together. Jeannie not so much."

"Were any of them friends with Chris Vogel or Kim Baskin?"

"I think Julie was friends with Kim."

"What do you know about Adam Renteria?"

"He's a dentist for children. I take my kids to him. Nice guy."

I thank her and write down the names. Then I call Professor Sharperson; he's in class but should be back in fifteen minutes.

Promptly fifteen minutes later, he calls me, and I ask my question. "Do you remember any of these people? Jeannie Wallace, Adam Renteria, and Julie Packard?"

He pauses for a few moments, no doubt trying to jog his memory. "I definitely knew Julie; she was in a couple of my classes. The other two sound familiar, but I can't place them."

"Would any of them have been in the clubs that you and Chris Vogel were in? Might they have heard him refer to himself as the King of Clubs?"

"I can't speak to what they might have heard. But I have no recollection of them being in our clubs. That's not to say it's not possible, but I would doubt it."

Nothing about this new information seems promising, which is why Laurie's talk about going on offense is sounding better and better.

"SAM HAS Z'S CELL PHONE NUMBER," LAURIE SAYS.

I turn to Sam. "How the hell did you get that? Never mind, I don't want to know; it must be illegal."

"Okay."

"All right, tell me how you got it." My curiosity has overcome my morality; that's becoming a common occurrence, which I'll have to analyze at some future date, maybe when my life is not in immediate jeopardy.

"It was fairly easy. The phone company computers know where cell phones are at all times because each one has a GPS in it."

"I know that."

"But it can also be reversed, meaning they can tell which cell phones are in a given place at a given time. So when the GPS monitor on Z's car said he was near Espinosa's office, I went into the phone company system and learned which cell phones were there at that particular time. There were eight of them.

"Then Z stopped at a diner, so I did the same thing; this time there were sixteen. Then he went back to the hotel, and I checked the cell phones there. There were a hundred and fourteen."

"And you found one phone common to all three places."

Sam nods. "Exactly. It has to be his phone; no one else would have followed exactly that pattern."

"That's brilliant."

"Aw, shucks."

"Totally illegal, but brilliant."

Laurie smiles; she knows how conflicted I am about these things. "All for a good cause."

"So how do we take advantage of this and go on offense?"

"We call Z; we tell him that we are willing to make a deal with Espinosa. We say we know we can't nail him for seven-year-old murders, and that we know he wouldn't have done it himself.

"So we say that we want to meet, and at that meeting he is to turn over the guy who actually committed the murders. Then he has to tell us where the bodies are, and that's all we care about. We get the killer and closure for the victims' families. He goes about his business, and we leave him alone."

"What does that accomplish? He's not going to go for that."

"Obviously not. But he'll claim to agree. We'll give him a time and location, and when we go there, he'll take his shot at us, at you. And this way we won't have to guess when he's coming; we'll know where and when and we'll be ready."

"He'll be ready also."

"We'll be readier because I've got a plan for that too. Either way, it's better than not knowing where or when he's coming."

"What if he just sends more goons?"

"Always possible," Laurie says. "But this will be a perfect opportunity for him; I don't think he'd want to miss it."

"Let me think about it for a while; I was hoping for something a little more brilliant. Make that much more brilliant." Then, "Okay, I'm in."

"That was fast," she says.

"I've got nothing better, and I'd like to get a decent night's sleep for a change. What's the phone number?"

"Let's figure out what you're going to say first."

So we do; we don't script it out, but we go over the main points. By the time we do, I've gone from being willing to go along with this to almost eager. I want to resolve this situation and move on.

Sam gives me the number and I dial it; a voice that I recognize as Z's answers on the first ring. "Yeah?" is his opening salvo.

"Z, how the hell are you? It's been a while; I haven't seen you since the park."

"You'll be seeing me again."

"I'm not interested in you; you're an asshole . . . you are shit on my shoe. It's your boss I want to see."

I go on to tell him our demands, that Espinosa turn over the killer and tell us where the bodies are. I set the meeting for tomorrow night at 9:00 P.M., at our favorite bench in Eastside Park.

"You got all that, little messenger boy?" I ask.

"I won't be forwarding your message. But I will be seeing you again."

"Nine P.M. tomorrow in the park."

I hang up as well and turn to Laurie. "I don't think he likes me, and I don't know if he'll be giving Espinosa the message. He said he wouldn't." Then, to Sam, "Can we find out what numbers he has called on that phone? Maybe it will tell us something."

"Of course. I should have done that already."

"Why would he say he won't give Espinosa the message? He should want us to be there; it gives Espinosa and him a shot at us."

"I don't know. But you said you had more to the plan, something that would help us prepare?"

Laurie nods. "Yup. And it might help us deal with getting the message across also. But it involves you making another phone call."

THIS CASE HAS CHANGED SUBSTANTIALLY FROM WHAT IT WAS ORIGINALLY supposed to be.

Our assignment was to solve a cold case; it wasn't to find a way to put a known criminal behind bars for being a known criminal. Maybe that's a better goal, and maybe jobs like that would make us "consultants" more productive, but it's not what we were hired to do.

In any event, that's where we are. We are never going to be able to prove that Espinosa killed Chris Vogel and Kim Baskin; the evidence to present to a jury will never exist. So the next best thing is to nail Espinosa for being Espinosa.

That's an outcome I can live with.

Joseph Russo, Jr., has agreed to meet with me at ten this morning, as Laurie knew he would. I've got a hunch this is a little early for him; Russo doesn't exactly have to punch a clock at the factory. But yesterday when I mentioned to his guy that I needed Russo's help putting Espinosa away, it must have turned him into a morning person.

Unfortunately, his eagerness did not extend to a willingness to have another get-together in Eastside Park. Instead he insisted on my coming to his house in the Riverside section of Paterson. Marcus wanted to come along, but I wouldn't let him. I'm not going to be in any danger; I'm offering something that Russo wants.

Espinosa.

Two large men are standing on the front steps in front of Russo's relatively modest house when I arrive. "I'm here to meet with Russo."

The guy on the left asks, "You carrying?"

"No."

I don't think he considers me to be trustworthy because he nods to his partner, who frisks me and confirms that I was telling the truth. Then they escort me inside to see their boss, who is wearing exercise clothes, sweatpants and a sweatshirt, as he sits watching television. Maybe he thinks that wearing the clothes is sufficient to stay in shape.

When he sees me, he says, "No rain and no grass."

I'm assuming he's still pissed off about having to meet in Eastside Park. "Very true. This is much more civilized. And much drier. And less green."

"So what the hell do you want now?"

He seems to forget that he called for the meeting last time, but I don't bother reminding him of that. Instead I tell him what has gone on between us and Espinosa.

When I get to the part about dealing with Glover and taking Espinosa's nine grand from him, Russo laughs. "You guys got guts, I'll give you that."

I then describe how we are trying to goad Espinosa by drawing him to this meeting, where we are hoping he will make his move.

He laughs again. "You guys got balls, I'll give you that."

"This is where you come in. You have an informant in Espinosa's operation. Someone high up."

His attitude immediately becomes wary. "Who told you that?"

"You did." I don't bother to mention that it was Laurie who figured it out. "When you told me that Vogel was talking to the Feds and Espinosa knew it. You had to have someone on the inside to give you that information."

"Keep talking."

"So I want information, in real time. I want to know how many people are coming and whether Espinosa will be one of them. I also want to know what they are planning, how they are going to make their move."

"If I did have someone in position to provide that information, doing this would make it impossible for him to continue to operate."

"Maybe, maybe not. But either way it's a small price to pay. You don't need anyone to spy on Espinosa if he's in prison for the rest of his life."

Russo thinks for a moment. "You could be right about that."

"And there's one other thing. The way we sent the message may not get through to Espinosa. I need your guy to deliver it as well. I've written out a note that your guy can say was left on the door of Espinosa's office."

"Anything else?" Russo asks, obviously annoyed.

"That's it. By tomorrow you can be living an Espinosa-free existence."

Russo thinks about that for a few moments. "How do you see this working?"

I describe what we need and he agrees. As meetings go, this was a good one.

I check my cell phone when I leave, and there is a message to call Sergeant Katy Seiffert. I had asked her to enter the playing card clue into the NCIC database.

I call her back and she says, "I put it into the system."

"Thanks. That was fast; I know how busy you are."

"I've got something that you're going to want to look at. You should come down here."

"Can it wait until tomorrow? I've sort of got a lot going on."

"It's been seven years, so I'm sure it can wait. But you definitely want to see this."

"I'll be down there tomorrow morning."

THE FIRST PHONE CALL COMES FROM SAM WILLIS, AT FIVE THIRTY THAT afternoon. I'm at Laurie's house with her and Marcus when it comes in.

"Z is at Espinosa's office. The GPS on the car and in his phone confirms it."

"No doubt?"

"One hundred percent certain that the car and phone are there. That's as much as I can tell you."

"Then Z must be part of it. Thanks, Sam."

I'm hoping that Z being personally involved doesn't mean that Espinosa won't be. But we should find that out soon enough. Also, based on Z's reputation, his being in the park will make tonight that much more dangerous.

It seems like the next half hour takes a week, but the second call, the important one, comes in at six o'clock, right on schedule. It's Joseph Russo, Jr. "According to my guy, there are six of them.

Espinosa is one of them. He's licking his chops at the chance to kill you."

"How will they come at us?"

"Nothing fancy. Two cars; Espinosa will be in the one that pulls into the park. The other one will park on Derrom Avenue, behind the trees. They'll come from that way, and they'll be firing at you from both sides. Remember Sonny at the tollbooth?"

He's referring to the scene in *The Godfather* in which the James Caan character got riddled with bullets. It's not a pleasant visual to call up right now.

"Will Z be with them?" I ask.

"The only one I know is Espinosa. Make sure you get him. If you get killed, I look bad."

"Then I'll try and stay alive."

"You do that." Click.

Assuming that Russo is correct, and it is certainly in his interest to be correct, then this is somewhat better than I thought. The police will handle the three guys that park on the street behind the trees. I just hope they can do it quietly, without gunfire, so that nothing scares Espinosa off.

Marcus and Laurie, with police backup, will outflank Espinosa and his pals when they come from the front. Hopefully they will do that before I get shot.

We'll get Espinosa for attempted murder, illegal possession of a firearm, and whatever other charges the prosecutors can come up with. I'm sure they'll think of some beauties.

I call Pete Stanton and explain the situation to him. He's been waiting to deploy his people, and he agrees that this setup is as good as we could have hoped for. The real danger is if Espinosa changes his tactics between now and nine o'clock, leaving us unprepared. I can't be at all sure that the new information would be conveyed to Russo, and then to me.

I call Dani to say hello and see how she is doing. I'm not going to tell her what is about to happen; I just want to hear her voice.

She asks me what is going on and says that she is anxious to come "home." I tell her that everything is fine and under control. I don't like deceiving her, but I just don't see any benefit to having her worrying all night.

After tonight's events I'll tell her everything that happened. Hopefully I'll also be able to tell her to come home. That is a phone call I really look forward to making.

Laurie and Marcus leave the house at eight o'clock to get in position. Andy is more nervous than we are, but Laurie assures him that all will be fine. I don't think he's convinced. He wants to come and help, but ultimately knows that Laurie is right when she says he might not be an asset to the operation. Andy with a gun would be a danger to good guys and bad guys alike.

I put on my bulletproof vest, leave, and am in position on the bench at eight forty-five. I know I am being watched and surrounded by a team of people, but I have rarely felt so alone.

I haven't brought Simon with me because everything will happen from a distance, so there will be no chance for him to employ his special skills. It wouldn't even be a help for him to detect them before they arrive; we'll know that well in advance. I also have absolutely no interest in him being in any potential line of fire.

I look at my watch about four or five hundred times between the time I get here and nine fifteen. I have no idea whether Espinosa is the type to be prompt; we don't socialize that much. But if he's thinking that being late will make me anxious, he's absolutely right about that. Adrenaline is sloshing around in my body like it's high tide.

What Espinosa couldn't realize, and what I am always struck by at times like this, is how much I relish these situations. We are going to be more than Espinosa can handle, and I'm going to enjoy watching him realize it.

I get a text from Pete saying that no one has appeared on Derrom Avenue either. The police are poised to arrest the group as soon as they get out of their cars; there is no way the police will let them enter the trees.

At nine twenty-five, my cell phone rings. I've had the ringer turned off and it is set to vibrate. I'm so tense that the sudden vibration feels like an earthquake. I look at the caller ID . . . it's Joseph Russo's number.

"Hello?"

"It's Russo. Espinosa ain't coming."

"Why not? Did your guy give him the message?"

"He gave it to him."

"So what happened?"

"Espinosa's dead; somebody shot him. That's all I know."

"Who shot him?"

"Which part of 'that's all I know' didn't you understand?"

I hang up and the phone rings again; this time it's Pete Stanton.

"I've got some news for you," he says.

"I know. Espinosa's dead."

"How the hell did you find that out?"

"I may have heard it from the guy who killed him."

LAURIE, MARCUS, AND I HEAD BACK TO LAURIE'S TO WATCH THE MEDIA reporting on Espinosa's murder.

It feels like going to a big sporting event and then watching television afterward to see the postgame coverage and interviews.

When we get there, Andy still has no idea what has happened. He's been watching for potential reporting on what we were planning in Eastside Park, but obviously there's been nothing about that, and also nothing yet about the Espinosa shooting.

It's another forty-five minutes before the first reports come on. Initially it's just that there has been a shooting, then that there is believed to be a single fatality, and finally that the victim is Espinosa, a reputed drug kingpin, and the gunman is at large.

Five minutes after the first mention of Espinosa, Dani calls me, having seen the reports. "Were you part of this?"

"No, we were supposed to be, but this cut our night short."

"Is he really dead?"

"I believe so, yes."

"Does it make me a bad person to say that I'm glad about it?"

"Nothing could make you a bad person. But if it makes you feel better, you can send flowers or a fruit basket to the service."

"I'm coming home now."

"I think it's better if you wait until tomorrow."

"You apparently didn't hear me clearly; I'm coming home now."

I know that tone; there is no way I am going to be able to talk her out of it, and no way I want to.

"I'm at Laurie's."

"Then I'm coming there."

Pete calls to say pretty much what we've already learned from the television coverage. A sniper's bullet hit Espinosa dead center in the chest as he was getting into his car. Everyone around him scattered, and no one was around when the police arrived on the scene. There is no suspect at the moment.

My initial thought had been that Russo must have had it done, but I'm rethinking it now. Laurie, Marcus, and Andy don't think it was him either.

"It wouldn't make sense," Andy says. "He could have tried to kill Espinosa at any time all these years, but he didn't want to take a chance on missing and starting a war. Now, when he knew you were just minutes from possibly taking Espinosa down, why would he do it? Russo is smarter than that."

"I agree," I say. "But if not Russo, then who?"

"Can't help you there; I don't know all the players. Maybe we'll have our answer when we see who takes over Espinosa's organization. Or maybe it was just someone who thought tonight was going to be a disaster and wanted to cut it off to save his own life."

Laurie nods. "If Russo had an informant in Espinosa's organization, maybe he in turn had one in Russo's. And maybe they reported in what was going to happen to someone below Espinosa, but rather than warn Espinosa, the guy saw it as a chance to get rid of him."

We're just wildly speculating, and none of this makes sense yet. Espinosa was in a dangerous business with violent people; he might have gotten shot for a reason that has nothing to do with us. I don't believe that to be the case; for it to have happened tonight would be a random coincidence, and as Professor Sharperson has pointed out, people don't behave randomly.

"I wonder if Z will take over," Andy says.

I shake my head. "I doubt it. He seems to have been a hired gun, but if one of his jobs was to protect Espinosa, then this is not going to look too good on his résumé."

"I'm not sure we have an assignment anymore," Laurie says. "We are sure that Espinosa killed Vogel and Baskin, or at least had them killed, and he's now out of the picture. Not sure what would be our purpose for staying on the case."

"We could find the bodies," I say. "We could find out who actually pulled the trigger. We could also find out why Kim Baskin died; I feel like she deserves that."

Laurie frowns. "I don't know how we do any of those things."

Dani shows up, which makes me want to get the hell out of here. She and I have a lot of catching up to do, verbally and otherwise.

Espinosa's dead, Dani's coming home, and I'm still alive. All in all, not a bad night . . . could have been a hell of a lot worse.

I'M NOT QUITE READY TO DROP THE VOGEL/BASKIN CASE.

We may know the who, meaning we know Espinosa was behind the killings, and we know the why, because Vogel was informing on him, but there is plenty more to learn. As I told Laurie, I still want to know who did the actual killing, whether directed to by Espinosa or not. Lastly, I want to find the bodies.

My first move today is going to see Sergeant Katy Seiffert. She told me she has something interesting to show me, something that I will definitely want to see. She's a pro and has been doing this for years; she wouldn't say that unless she came up with something that could be important.

Katy generally doesn't waste any time on small talk, one of the things I like about her. "Your instincts were right. Putting the king of clubs into the NCIC data bank may have been too specific. I put it in that way again, just to test it out and see if it's been updated, and again came up with nothing. But when I put in *single playing card,* it was a different story."

"What did you get?"

"There have been four murders in the past twelve years, not including Vogel and Baskin, in which a single playing card was found at the scene."

"Whoa . . . where were they?"

She reads off a list. "A seventy-nine-year-old woman in Omaha, a forty-eight-year-old woman who was a hospital employee in Detroit, a thirty-two-year-old male mechanic in Boulder, and a sixty-one-year-old male insurance salesman in Jacksonville."

"Anything obvious in common?"

"You mean besides the fact that they were all killed?"

I smile. "Yes. Besides that."

"Well, all the cases are listed as unsolved, so there's that. I really haven't studied them in any detail, but I've printed out all the case reports. You can certainly talk to the supervising detectives; their names are in the reports."

I thank Katy and take all the information home with me. On the way I call Laurie and tell her about this development, and she considers it as potentially significant as I do.

"I'll know more when I dive into it," I say. "And that will start the second I get home."

I'm not fully true to my word; I don't start right away. Instead I take Simon for a walk; I haven't been paying as much attention to him as I should, and walking with him helps me clear my head and think.

When we get home, I open the reports, but if I had expected a bombshell, I would be disappointed. Nothing in any of this paperwork hints at a motive that the killers could have had, and none of these people are known to have any enemies or connection to violent criminals.

They also have no obvious connection to each other, though that was not analyzed by the individual investigators. That's because they didn't know about the other cases. Hopefully when I get into it, I'll find some connections, but that seems unlikely.

A seventy-nine-year-old retired woman in Omaha and a thirty-two-year-old mechanic in Boulder? A forty-eight-year-old hospital worker in Detroit and a sixty-one-year-old insurance salesman in Jacksonville? If something ties them together, it sure as hell doesn't jump out of these reports.

As Katy said, in each case a playing card was found near the body. But even the cards seem unrelated . . . a four of diamonds, a six of spades, a seven of hearts, a nine of diamonds, and of course the king of clubs from the Vogel and Baskin murders.

In none of the cases did the detectives assign any particular importance to the playing card; they just dutifully and properly reported it into the system. I wonder if there were other murders in which the cops were not quite so diligent and did not input the information. That is possible, maybe even probable.

Even with this quick look, two differences between all these cases and Vogel/Baskin are obvious. One is the number of victims: our case is the only one in which more than one person died. The other difference is that in the other four murders, the bodies were not hidden; they were all found at the scene.

But there is way too much here to dismiss this; it's going to have to be analyzed, and we're going to need to talk to the detectives in the four cities.

I call Sam Willis and give him all of the relevant information. I ask him if he can work his cyber magic and find any connections among the victims, with special attention on Chris Vogel and Kim Baskin. If they had anything to do with these other people, I want to know about it.

"CHECK YOUR MAILBOX."

It's a voice I don't recognize; it might even be computer masked. The caller ID had said *private caller,* and the entire conversation consisted of my "Hello" and then just those three words, after which he hung up.

My inclination when someone tells me to check my mailbox is to check my mailbox, but in this case it's not quite that simple. Since I don't know who called, and the situation is at best quite suspicious, the box could be booby-trapped.

Most people in this situation would call the police and get the bomb squad to come out. That's because most people in this situation don't have a live-in buddy like Simon. Part of his training was explosives detection, and he is extremely good at it.

I tell Dani that I'm taking Simon for a quick walk. I don't tell her that we'll be back in a couple of minutes or not at all. It seems like I spend half my time not telling Dani about life-threatening things that I'm doing; maybe that's a sign that I should adjust my lifestyle.

I bring Simon over to the mailbox so that he can sniff for explosives. He doesn't react at all, so I'm pretty sure we're fine. Just to be sure, I bring him back to the house and out of harm's way. Then I grab a broom and head back out.

"You're going outside to sweep?" Dani asks.

"Sort of."

"You are full of surprises."

I go to the mailbox again. Just because I'm confident it's not going to blow up, that doesn't mean it's not dangerous. For all I know there can be a gun set to go off or an open jar of anthrax or a dozen poisonous snakes. Fortunately, no neighbors are out and about, so if something happens and gets out of control, I won't have to go on trial for murder by mailbox.

I take a deep breath, stand to the side, and stick out the broom to slowly and carefully open the door handle. Most of the neighbors already consider me insane, and if they are watching me from their windows, this will confirm it for them.

Once the door falls open and nothing happens, I cautiously walk over and look inside. There is a single piece of paper, with printed words on it in computer type.

I go back in the house, return the broom, grab a napkin, and head outside again. Dani sees me but doesn't say anything; she has to be quite sure that I've lost my mind. I use the napkin to pick up the paper by the corner, so as not to disturb any potential fingerprints.

I carry it inside and place it on a table. I still haven't read it, and Dani comes over to see what it is.

"This was in the mailbox."

We start to read it together.

"Holy shit."

I couldn't have said it any better myself.

The first line is *Here's where the bodies are buried*. If headlines are supposed to get you to read the story under it, this one is effective.

I call Laurie to tell her what's happened, and she calls Pete. Within fifteen minutes he is here with a full forensics team, to check the note and my mailbox for fingerprints and DNA.

The note describes an area in Pennington Park, in the Great Falls Historic District in Paterson. It even has a hand-drawn map, which clearly shows where in a wooded area behind the baseball field the bodies are supposedly buried.

Pete sends in a team that is apparently expert in these kind of things, as well as more forensics people. Once the forensics officers in our house have finished with the note, they head to the park as well.

I pick up Laurie and Andy and we follow the police down to Pennington Park. By the time we get there, the place is crawling with cops and the area has been roped off. If this was an attempt by someone to draw me into some kind of ambush, it didn't work out so well. By my rough count, there are probably twenty heavily armed police officers; if this contingent were at the Alamo, Davy Crockett would today be selling coonskin caps on the Shopping Network.

There is also excavating equipment, and shovels abound, but we stand around for at least an hour before anyone does anything. It's like they are planning the D-day invasion. I don't get it; they've got shovels, they might as well start digging.

They've also got dogs; I should have brought Simon. I can't tell what the dogs are doing, but it most likely includes sniffing for explosive booby traps, as well as for cadavers. They keep us about twenty-five feet away, which is a little annoying, since it's my mailbox that started the whole thing.

Finally the digging begins, but slowly and painstakingly. There's a chance this could be a scam, but I don't know what anyone would gain from that. But I also don't know what anyone would gain by telling us where the bodies are.

All of a sudden there is some increased activity, though I can't tell what is happening.

After another fifteen minutes, Pete Stanton comes over to us. "It looks like they've found two bodies. No confirmed identity yet, but I think we can make a pretty good guess."

"Do you know how they died?" Laurie asks.

"Not yet."

Pete leaves, and I say, "Well, they are clearly not in the witness protection program. If they are, the program needs some serious revamping."

"A murder-suicide is also out the window," Andy says. "Pretty hard to bury your own body."

There's nothing left for us to do here, so I drop Laurie and Andy off at home. But I'm not going straight home; I've got another stop to make.

And I'm dreading it.

"MISS CREWS, IT'S COREY DOUGLAS. CAN I COME IN?"

"Oh, of course." She buzzes me into the building. I take the elevator to her apartment, and she is at the open door, in her wheelchair, waiting for me.

"I didn't expect you to come see me again. But of course you're always welcome. I get very few visitors these days."

"I'm sorry to barge in like this, but I need to talk to you."

"Please come in."

She spends some time offering me coffee and cake and telling me about her neighbor's cat being lost. I think she is dreading hearing what I have to say and is putting it off. I'm looking forward to it even less than she is.

Finally, I get to it. "Miss Crews, something has happened that you need to know about."

"They found my Chris." It's more of a statement than a question.

"I think so, yes. They're not sure yet; they're running tests. I didn't want you to have to hear it on television. I'm very sorry."

"And that poor girl also?"

"Yes."

She is quiet for a while. For a few moments I think she is going to break down crying, but then she seems to compose herself. "It's better to know. Not knowing is terrible. So many years . . ."

"I wish I had better news."

"It's not your fault; you're a good person, and I appreciate your coming here. I'm sure that was hard for you to do."

"Are you okay? Can I do anything for you?"

"I'm fine; don't worry about me. Will you find out who did this to my Chris?"

"I hope so; I'll certainly try. Can I ask you a question?"

"Certainly."

I mention the names of the four people that were murdered and had playing cards left at the scene. I don't say that they were murder victims; nor do I say where they lived. I just ask her if Chris had ever mentioned any of those names.

"No, not to me. Did Chris know them?"

"I don't think so, but I wanted to make sure. Their names came up during the investigation . . . probably nothing important."

We talk a little more and then I leave. She thanks me again, though all I did was add a little more misery to her life.

I cannot figure out who might have revealed where the bodies were buried, or what they had to gain by doing so. It's almost as if with Espinosa dead, someone wanted to wipe the slate clean. It certainly seems like his death somehow triggered the revelation.

Maybe it is someone in his organization who wants our investigation to end because they might also be culpable. The reasoning would be that with the perpetrator, Espinosa, gone, and the bodies discovered, there is no reason for us to continue our involvement.

They may well be logically correct.

But logic has never gotten in our way before, and there is a huge list of things that I still want to know.

I want to know everything that happened the night of the reunion.

I want to know if the four deaths with playing-card clues around the country are related to this case.

I want to know who killed Espinosa.

I want to know how Z fits into all this.

I want to know what was the source of Chris Vogel's income, and who was wiring money to him.

And now I want to know why the location of the bodies was revealed.

In short, I want to know everything.

Z is particularly interesting. He is known to have performed his violent trade in other areas of the country; could he be responsible for those four deaths? And is leaving a playing card a calling card, his personal gimmick?

But if he was responsible, was he working for different people each time? Why would Espinosa possibly have any interest in killing a seventy-nine-year-old retired woman in Omaha? Or any of those other people?

Maybe they were murders that Z was hired to commit by different employers. He left his calling card at the scenes, perhaps a conceit that he thought people wouldn't connect.

Or maybe the playing cards are meaningless. Maybe with all the murders that have been committed in this country in the past decade, four of them having playing cards at the scene is statistically inevitable. Could that be?

I call Pete Stanton to see if they have learned any more from the scene in Pennington Park.

"No ironclad identifications yet. But you can bet it's them."

"I'm sure you're right. By the way, I told Vogel's mother what is going on. I don't know anyone in Baskin's family."

"We'll have people handle that once a definite identification is made. Oh, one more thing."

"What's that?"

"There was a playing card buried with Baskin's body. A queen of diamonds."

I SPEND AN ENTIRE MORNING, AND PART OF THE AFTERNOON, CONTACTING the detectives who handled the murder cases in the other four cities.

It's not easy to reach them, and the only one I get right away is the guy in Jacksonville. The detective in Omaha has since retired, but I speak to the lieutenant who was in second position on the case. After a few hours, the detective in Boulder calls me back, but I still haven't reached anyone in Detroit.

By the time I'm finished, I know almost nothing more than when I started. There seems to be no connection between the victims, and no similarities other than the fact that in none of the cases were the cops able to come up with a possible motive.

The woman in Omaha was killed in her house, and it seemed to have been ransacked, but the police thought the robbery part of it was staged. In the other two cases no possible motives at all were identified.

None of the victims had any significant drug involvement, though one of them had marijuana in his home. It was not a large amount, indicating that the man was a casual user, and certainly not a seller. And even that was not stolen by the killer.

Also, the method of murder was different in each case. There was a strangulation, a shooting, a stabbing, and a drowning in a bathtub. No forensics were found to tie anyone to any of them; whoever did these killings, whether it was one person or more, was a pro.

In all the cases, the cops found the playing card to be curious, but couldn't come up with any reason for it. Nor could they determine if it was significant. It was just one piece to a puzzle that they couldn't come close to solving.

But there is no longer a possibility that Vogel carried the king of clubs to make some kind of statement about what he called himself in high school. The presence of a card on Baskin's buried body precludes that. The cards are absolutely significant.

Sam Willis calls me with a disturbing piece of news: Z has disappeared. He checked out of the hotel, but left his phone behind. He took his car with him, but apparently found and detached the GPS.

Again, as with just about everything else in this case, a number of explanations are possible for his going off the grid. Maybe it's as simple as the fact that with his employer dead, Z has no reason to hang around. He's a hired gun, so maybe he's left to go where he can make money.

Or maybe Z's scared. Maybe he was so tied in to Espinosa that he fears that whoever killed him will now come for Z.

Or maybe Z is the one who killed Espinosa. Maybe they had a falling out over money or whatever, and Z decided he had had enough. The deadly accurate single rifle shot from a distance is consistent with Z's abilities.

Or maybe Z got married and he and his wife opened a hardware store in Topeka, and the ribbon cutting was yesterday.

As long as Z is still on the loose, I remain worried about Dani. Not as much as before, but I'm glad Bill Sampson is still watching out for her.

Between Laurie and me, we interview the three people who left the reunion without picking up their gift bags.

I speak to Dr. Adam Renteria in his dentist office, with screaming kids everywhere. It's amazing to me that anyone would choose to do what he does, no less go to school for years to do it.

I hated going to the dentist as a kid, much like I hate going to the dentist as an adult. But if I yelled and carried on like these kids, then I deserved to get treated without Novocain.

Renteria remembers the reunion and certainly remembers the disappearance of Vogel and Baskin. He has absolutely no recollection as to whether he took a gift bag and seems amused by the question.

"Am I being accused of stealing a reunion gift bag?" He smiles. "Are you here to take me into custody?"

Just then a particularly loud scream comes from one of the children in the waiting room. "No, you've clearly suffered enough."

PETE STANTON HANDLES THE NEWS CONFERENCE TO ANNOUNCE THAT THE bodies of Chris Vogel and Kim Baskin have been found.

He says that positive identifications have been made, and that the remains are consistent with their having died seven years ago, around the time of their disappearance from the reunion. He also says that each victim died of a single gunshot wound to the head. He does not say anything about how the police learned the location of the bodies.

Also, no mention is made of the playing card found on Kim Baskin's body, just like there was never a public revelation of the king of clubs being found in the car. Cases like this often draw fake confessions, and the information about the cards could be used to determine if a confession is legit.

When Pete opens up the session to questions, reporters obviously ask him about the search for the killers. Pete deflects most of them by using the old standby that he can't comment on an ongoing investigation, but he does surprise me by saying the police have identified a person of interest.

He doesn't mention Espinosa, though I know that is who he is talking about. He also doesn't say that the person of interest was himself murdered a few days ago. But maybe Pete is going to ultimately declare the cold case solved.

I have to admit that we are running out of investigative leads. I'd love to know where Z is, but I have no way of finding him short of running into him in a shopping mall.

The New Jersey state cop, D'Antoni, told us Z had previously not been seen in years; he has the skill set that would enable him to disappear at will. I can't say I'm thrilled about the idea of Z being out there, looking for revenge against me. Maybe I shouldn't have called him "asshole" and "little messenger boy."

Enter Sam Willis to the rescue.

Sam calls a meeting at Laurie's to tell us some information he has come up with. He could have just told Laurie or me over the phone, but Sam has a flare for the dramatic.

I bring Simon over, and Laurie and I await Sam's arrival. He gets here ten minutes late, which is uncharacteristic of him.

"Sorry. More information keeps coming in."

"What kind of information?" Laurie asks. Sam has a habit of dribbling out whatever he has to say, so precise questioning is necessary to speed him up and keep him on point.

"I've been trying to connect Chris Vogel to any of the victims in these four cities. It's really hard to do. I mean, let's say he took one of them to dinner; if he paid the check, or if the other person did, how would I know that they were together?"

"So you didn't connect them?" Laurie asks.

"No, but I found something else just as good. Maybe better."

"I think we're ready to hear what that is," I say.

"Chris Vogel visited three of the four cities, anywhere from three weeks to one week before the murders. He stayed an average of three days in each city. And the murder in the city he didn't visit, Detroit, happened three years after he died."

"Holy shit," I say, and if anything, that is understating the case.

Sam has made a chart, showing the three cities, the days Vogel was there, and the dates of the murders. If this is a coincidence, it's the hugest one of all time.

"Did he stay in hotels?"

"Yes, in all three of the cases they were airport hotels. He was not in these places on sightseeing vacations."

"Sam, did he travel a lot, other than in these instances?" Laurie asks.

"No, just a few other times."

"Can you give us the information on those other trips?"

She's thinking what I'm thinking, that if Vogel is tied to these murders, then maybe we can learn if there were more of them. Maybe playing cards were not left at the scene, or perhaps they were and just weren't correctly fed by the detectives into the NCIC data bank.

Sam promises to get right on this additional information, leaving Laurie and me to discuss what this new revelation means. Andy comes into the room, and we tell him what has just happened.

Andy doesn't beat around the bush. "Your boy isn't just a murder victim; he's also a murderer."

"He wasn't there when they were committed," Laurie says, "but I take your point. He could well have been an accomplice."

"He was checking out the scene, preparing the killer for what he was going to have to deal with," I say. "I can't think of another explanation."

"But why? What would he have to gain from this?" Laurie asks.

"Money. But among the things I don't understand is why a killer would pick Chris Vogel to be his front man."

I don't have an answer to that, so I call Peter Hauser, Vogel's manager at the automobile dealership. I ask him if Vogel traveled a lot and therefore missed work because of it.

"Not really. Not compared to my other salesman. He'd go off for four or five days at a time, but if he did it once a year, that would be a lot."

"Did he say what he was doing, or where he was going?"

"No, but I remember being surprised once. He said he was staying home for a few days, taking vacation time, but I needed to call and ask him something about a potential sale. I didn't get him, so I left a message, but he called me back from a hotel phone number in Omaha.

"It was so strange that I asked him why he was there, and he said it was a family emergency. I didn't know he had any family in Omaha, but I didn't push it."

Laurie and I kick it around for a while and get nowhere. I suggest that she and I once again contact the detectives in these towns, send them a photograph of Vogel, and ask if he had come up in their investigations.

She agrees, not because she thinks anything will come out of it, but more because it will give the illusion that we are doing something productive.

I take Boulder and Omaha, and Laurie takes Jacksonville.

Here goes nothing.

NONE OF THE DETECTIVES IN THE THREE CITIES KNOW ANYTHING ABOUT Chris Vogel.

He did not come up in their investigations, at least not to their knowledge, but each says they will look into it further. I'm not surprised by this; we are talking about more than seven years ago, and about a person who was not even in their cities when the murders were committed.

They all promise to get back to us if they learn anything else. I'm sure they're well-intentioned, but if they're like every other cop everywhere, then they have current matters to worry about. It's also not important that we hear from them; we already know that Vogel was in their towns. That is the crucial point; whether he came to the investigators' attention is not.

A few hours later an email comes in from Lieutenant Jake Broyles in Omaha. He wasn't the lead on the case, but has been my contact because the detective who was in charge has since retired. He tells me that there is someone I should talk to, and he has set up a Zoom call at 3:00 P.M. for me to do so.

"Dani!" I scream. It's not a panicked scream, but close.

She comes into the room immediately. "What's wrong?"

"I need to be on a Zoom call at three o'clock."

"And?"

"I have no idea how."

She shakes her head at the pathetic aspect of it all. "Did they send you a link?"

"I don't know. Where would it be?"

She looks at the email on my computer. "They did. I can show you what to do, or I can come in at three P.M. and do it for you."

"Guess which one I pick."

"See you at three."

I call Laurie and tell her what's going on, and she says that she'll come over at that time. She knows how to set up a Zoom call, so I am able to let Dani off the hook, which saves me from further humiliation.

Before I know it, we're looking at a computer screen with Lieutenant Broyles in one square, me in another, and a woman he introduces as Beth Ashford in a third. Beth looks to be in her midfifties.

"Beth's mother is Lillian Ashford," Broyles says. "She was the murder victim; eight years ago someone broke into her house and drowned her in the bathtub. The house had the appearance of being ransacked, but nothing was found to be missing, and it's our considered opinion that the scene was staged.

"I've shown Beth the photograph that you sent me of Chris Vogel, and she recognized him. I'll let her describe her experience. Beth?"

Beth doesn't beat around the bush. "I met him, about three weeks before my mother died. I'm almost certain of it."

"What were the circumstances?" I ask.

"My mother had an apartment above her detached garage. She rented it out, but a long-term renter had left, so it was on the market again. This man came to see it, with the possibility of renting it. I was at my mother's when he showed up. I remember it like it was yesterday."

"Did he say how long he wanted to rent it for?"

"Yes, at least a year. But there was something strange about him."

"Strange how?"

"I can't put my finger on it. But he made me uncomfortable, and it's why I remember him. For one thing, he didn't seem that interested in the particulars of the apartment. Whatever she said, he just nodded, but I don't think he was listening."

"Where did he leave it? Did he take the apartment?"

"What happened was, while he was there, I took my mother aside and said she should not let him take it. She also had an uneasy feeling about him. So when she was finished showing it, she said that there were other people coming to look at it, and she would let him know. I don't think he cared either way."

"Did you or she ever hear from him again?"

Beth shakes her head. "No, I don't think so. Mom asked how she could reach him, and he said that it would be difficult, and that he would call her. I'm pretty sure he never did."

"Did she rent it to someone else?"

"She never got the chance; she died three weeks later."

"I'm sorry."

"Thank you. Oh, there's one other thing that I forgot to tell you. He didn't give his name as Vogel. He said his last name was Chance. I'm fairly sure he called himself Richard Chance."

Chance. The nickname that was shown in the high school yearbook. That removes any doubt that the person she remembers was really Chris Vogel.

I thank her, and after promising to keep both of them informed if we get a break in their case, I break off the call.

I look at Laurie and she says, "There is no question about it. Chris Vogel was part of a conspiracy to commit murder."

LAURIE WAS RIGHT, BUT SHE UNDERSTATED THE CASE.

Chris Vogel does not seem only to have been part of a conspiracy to commit murder, but rather a conspiracy to commit multiple murders. At least four, maybe more. Maybe even his own.

It is extremely frustrating that I am no closer to knowing what happened after that reunion than I was when I started. My guess is that Kim Baskin was meant to be a victim all along, but I can't be sure of that. I think Chris Vogel was setting her up, but something went wrong with his plan, and he became a victim as well.

Did he find a conscience at the last minute, possibly try to save Baskin, thereby ensuring his own demise along with hers? That seems unlikely based on how many murders went before it, but it can't be completely discounted.

Or was he the intended victim all along, the result of an argument among the conspirators, and Baskin happened to be in the wrong place at the wrong time?

One thing we know with certainty is that Z was working for Espinosa, but it's hard to connect Espinosa to murders in Omaha, Jacksonville, et cetera. The victims in those cities were apparently not involved in the drug trade, and even if they had been, Espinosa had no operations there. Why would he want them dead?

It would seem that Z must have had different employers in each of those cities, all of whom hired him to commit the murders. And Z could have somehow had a long-standing relationship with Vogel, who helped him plan the murders. In this shaky theory, they were coconspirators.

But then Espinosa just happens to hire Z to kill Z's coconspirator, Vogel, because he was informing on Espinosa to the Feds? Are there coincidences that big?

We don't have the time, and certainly not the wherewithal, to do an in-depth investigation of the murders in the other cities. But they seem to have not been spur-of-the-moment killings. They were well planned, as evidenced by Vogel's traveling and doing what seems to have been scouting missions.

These things happen for a reason. In each case, someone had to have a specific goal or objective in mind that was advanced by the murder. Someone hired Vogel and the actual killer, probably Z, to do the jobs. They would not have come cheap, especially Z.

I had hoped I'd make it through the rest of my life without ever talking to Joseph Russo, Jr., again, but why would I be so lucky? I once again call the number that his guy originally called me from, and the same voice answers.

"This is Corey Douglas. I need to speak to Joseph Russo."

"What about?"

"It's personal. Can you put him on the phone?"

"Mr. Russo doesn't speak on the phone."

"Ever? Is that like a thing with him? Like I don't eat broccoli?"

I don't think the guy appreciates the analogy because he says he may or may not call me back and hangs up.

Ten minutes later he calls back. "Mr. Russo will see you in an hour."

"Eastside Park?"

"No." Click.

I call Laurie to tell her what's going on, mainly so she'll know who to blame if I'm never heard from again, though I decide not to alert Dani. Then I head down to Russo's house, get frisked, and am brought in to see the great one exactly one hour from the time I got off the phone with his guy.

He's dressed in what seems to be the same sweatpants and sweatshirt; I can't tell if they've been washed, but I'm glad I'm here to talk to him and not slow dance with him.

"I see you more than my mother," he says, revealing either an unexpected sense of humor or a callous disregard for Mama Russo.

"She must be very proud." Then, "I need to talk to the guy you have in Espinosa's operation."

"Why is that?"

"I'm trying to solve a case."

"And I'm trying to figure out why I should give a shit that you're trying to solve a case."

"Espinosa's operation will continue on without him. Somebody else will just pick up where he left off. I might be able to blow it up entirely."

"How?"

Since what I said was a complete lie, I avoid the question with "I can't go there now. But since I got involved, Espinosa's gone, so I should get credit for a good track record so far."

"If my man is seen talking to you, he's as good as dead."

"I have a solution for that."

"Then you better tell me what it is."

So I do.

DETECTIVES WORKING FOR PETE STANTON BRING CHUCKIE PARRATTO AND Billy Soto in for questioning regarding the murder of Espinosa.

It's a scam; Pete has no particular interest in questioning them. And while he would never admit this, probably the only reason he would want to catch Espinosa's killer would be to thank him.

Parratto is belligerent and uncooperative when brought in, as is Soto. The main difference is that Soto is faking that attitude; he is Russo's informant and Russo has told him what is going on. He has been brought in for questioning, but it's me who will be doing it.

Pete's guys leave me alone with him. They could certainly be listening in through microphones if they're so inclined; I don't care either way.

"Russo told you what's going on?"

"He said to talk to you." Soto's attitude is sullen and annoyed; maybe he wasn't faking it. I get that a lot.

"Good . . . it's about Espinosa's operation."

He doesn't say anything, though he could have said, *Really, Captain Obvious?*

"Do you know who shot him?"

"No, but I'm glad the guy isn't shooting at me. He had to be at least two hundred feet away. Probably more. One shot blew a hole in his chest the size of the Lincoln goddamn Tunnel."

I hand him a picture of Z. "What can you tell me about this guy?"

He looks at it for about ten seconds. "Nothing. Who is he?"

"He goes by Z. You've never seen him?"

"Never."

"He worked for Espinosa. He was with him when he got shot."

"Bullshit. I was with him, and I'm telling you I've never seen this guy."

I don't know where to go with this; Sam told me that based on the GPS in Z's phone and car, he was with Espinosa that night and had been with him a number of times before.

"Could he have been there and you didn't see him?"

"Maybe if he was hiding under the desk, but other than that, no."

"Who is running Espinosa's operation now?"

"Hasn't been fully decided yet, but it looks like Emile Mateo. He's going at it damn hard, which means he'd be happy to kill anyone who isn't on his side."

"Could Mateo have killed Espinosa?"

"Not personally; he was with us that night when it happened. But he could have had it done; who wouldn't want the top job?"

"I wouldn't, but I've always been lacking in ambition. So you don't know who pulled the trigger?"

He shakes his head and then points to Z's picture. "Can this guy shoot?"

"So they say."

I turn Soto over to Pete, who in turn releases him and Parratto, who has been forced to field actual questions about the Espinosa murder. I think that overall our plan has been handled well and left no one with a reason to question Soto's loyalty. Laurie and I are going to wait in the precinct a while to meet with Pete as soon as he handles a few internal things he has going on.

If Sam is right about the GPS signals, and I've never known Sam to be wrong . . . and if Soto is right that Z was not with Espinosa that night . . . then Z must have been the one who killed him.

There can't be any other explanation, especially since the accuracy of the shooter so neatly fits in to Z's reputed skill set.

Maybe Espinosa and Z had a boss-employee falling out, just like the apparent falling out between Espinosa and Vogel.

Or it's possible that Mateo offered more than Z was getting from Espinosa and decided to remove this barrier to the top job. I haven't spent a lot of time with Z, but I've got a hunch that loyalty is not his defining quality.

The most likely scenario is that Z was cleaning up loose ends and considered it time to move on with nothing left behind to tie him into any of this.

With all the questions surrounding everything connected to this case, one thing is absolutely certain.

A lot of people die when Z is around.

SAM WILLIS IS WORTH HIS WEIGHT IN COMPUTER CHIPS.

I have no idea why this guy is not working for the CIA, or maybe he is and is just moonlighting for us. But he is definitely a keeper.

He calls my cell while Laurie and I are waiting to meet with Pete. Even though I had not thought to tell him to do so, he has been scouring local hotels to see if the fake ID that Z had been using, Steven LaRusso, turned up anywhere.

It has.

Z may well not have had access to a different fake ID, and he wouldn't have any way of knowing that we knew which name he was using. But his using it again was an uncharacteristic error, and Sam caught him on it.

The killer formerly known as LaRusso is staying at a hotel down toward central New Jersey, near where the New Jersey Turnpike and Garden State Parkway intersect. It's an interesting and smart choice; if he had to leave in a hurry, he could drive in either direction on either major highway, making him much more difficult to follow.

It's also far enough away from the North Jersey area that he has terrorized to make him feel safe from detection. Of course, he was not aware of the prowess of one Sam Willis.

The most interesting part of this is that Z has remained in the area at all, since he has never been known to have a dedicated home base. If this area has become dangerous to him, and he clearly must think it is, then why stay around here at all? The simple, worrisome answer is that he must have more to do.

When Pete is ready for us, we go in to update him on the status of the case. It's likely that we have accomplished all we are going to, and since he's paying the freight, he has a right to weigh in on where we go from here.

We bring Pete up-to-date, starting with the murders we've uncovered that Vogel was apparently connected to in three of the four other cities. He's off the hook on the fourth one, because he was dead at the time.

Pete is clearly shocked by this and has a lot of questions, only some of which we can answer. But he certainly doesn't question that Vogel's being in each of those cities shortly before the murders can't be a coincidence.

I move on to tell him about my conversation with Soto, Russo's guy, who credibly claimed not to have ever seen Z. We also tell him about having located Z, though we don't tell him how. No sense throwing Sam under the legal bus, even if Pete probably already knows the work he does for Andy.

"I have to admit that cold cases don't stay cold for long when you guys get involved," he says. "You have done damn good work."

"The question is . . . do you want us to continue?" Laurie asks.

"Why are you asking that?"

"Because we may well be running into a brick wall. Espinosa ordered the killing of Vogel and Baskin; we're pretty sure of that. Z probably did it, but it's unlikely we could ever prove it. And even if Vogel was involved in multiple murders, including Baskin's and maybe even his own, he and Espinosa are obviously never going to face trial."

"So?"

"So you're paying us, and if we're not going to get anywhere, then you have the right to stop doing so," I say.

He thinks for a few moments. "As far as consultants go, you're a very noble group. Let me ask you this. If I take you off the case and stop paying, are you going to keep at it, or are you going to drop it?"

"Keep at it," Laurie and I say at the same time.

Pete smiles. "That's what I thought. I'll keep paying."

An idea hits me. "Actually, since we're still on the payroll, we can use your help."

LAURIE, MARCUS, WILLIE, AND I HAVE BEEN TAKING TURNS WATCHING THE hotel Z is staying at. The only times he has left have been each day at around noon, to go to a diner and sometimes a supermarket.

For a notorious bad guy, he is living a pretty normal life.

We have taken advantage of this time for Sam Willis to once again zero in on Z's phone. It's a breeze for Sam; he just searched the phone company database for phones that were in the hotel and diner when Z was in each place. Once he got a match, we knew Z's number.

I've told Sam to once again find out if Z has called anyone, and if so, who. Last time it didn't get us anything, but we live in hope.

Today is the day we are planning to make our move, so I assign myself the job of watching for him. Sure enough, at twenty to one, he comes out, gets in his car, and drives off.

I call Pete Stanton, and he calls his contact at the Middlesex

County Sheriff's Office. They send four officers in two sedans, rather than a police car. We don't want Z to see what is going on and take off.

Z takes longer than usual to get back, which is just as well, since it takes Pete a while to get here with two of his detectives and two other officers.

We watch as Z parks his car and heads for the door to the hotel, at which point the Middlesex officers move in. "Excuse me," one of the officers says. "We would like to talk to you."

Z looks at them warily, but doesn't bolt. He's too smart for that. "What's the problem, Officer?"

"You're wanted for questioning in Paterson for the murder of Espinosa. Will you come along voluntarily?"

"No."

"Is your name Steven LaRusso?"

"Yes."

"Did you use that name to board an airplane six weeks ago?"

"No."

Pete and the Paterson cops have moved in. "Lying to an officer . . . twice. That's not a good sign." He points to a bulge in Z's jacket. "Neither is that."

Two cops draw their weapons, and Z is instructed to place his hands behind his head. He complies, and one of the officers removes a gun from Z's pocket.

"Do you have a license to carry this in New Jersey?"

"I have nothing to say to you."

"Well, you are heading to Paterson." The officer turns to Pete. "You want to take over?"

"With pleasure."

When I see that Pete has taken possession of the prisoner, I walk over. Z clearly reacts to seeing me. "Hello, little messenger boy," I say. "So nice to see you again."

Z is placed into one of the Paterson cars, but a detective stays behind. He is going to work with the Middlesex cops to get a warrant to search Z's hotel room and car. The illegal possession of a firearm will allow them to do that, the theory being that they are looking for more weapons. They won't have trouble getting a judge to sign that.

I call Alvarez at the DEA and alert him that Z is in our control. He has pulled some strings with Homeland Security and secured a request for the local Paterson cops to hold Z for the illegal use of a fake ID on an airplane.

Things are moving right along.

I head back to the Paterson police station in my car and call Laurie on the way so she can meet me there. We'll watch the questioning of Z over the closed-circuit system.

Detective Larry Summerfield, who Pete says is his best interrogator, enters the room where the handcuffed Z is waiting. If Z is intimidated, he's hiding it well; his expression is smug and confident.

"Well, hello, Leonard." Summerfield uses Z's actual first name. I assume he thinks it might unnerve and annoy Z, but it doesn't seem to.

"Talk quickly. I won't be here long."

"We already have you for lying to a police officer, illegal possession of a weapon, using a fake ID to board an airplane . . . you'll be our guest for a while."

Z just laughs. "You'd better have more than that."

"Oh, we will. Let's talk about Chris Vogel and Kim Baskin."

"Who? I can't place the names."

"You remember Vogel. He was your traveling companion."

If this was designed to draw a reaction from Z, it didn't work. He just smiles. "You might be able to place Vogel in those places, but not me. Sorry."

The rest of the session goes nowhere. Summerfield turns the conversation to Espinosa, but Z deflects it easily. He knows that the three charges are all the cops have, and that will not be enough to keep him in custody.

Z will make bail, and then he will disappear, and he'll never be heard from again. We have not accomplished much other than putting this on Z's record in the event that he's taken into some future custody.

What I am most interested in is the result of the search warrant on Z's hotel room. That was a key goal here, and I'm hoping there's something there that can put Z away.

It would also be nice if it tells us what the hell has been going on.

THE SEARCH OF Z'S HOTEL ROOM AND CAR DOES NOT GIVE US WHAT WE want, but it scares the hell out of me.

There is nothing at all that could be considered incriminating; Z is obviously too smart for that. I can only assume that he anticipated the possibility that the authorities would move in and made sure they'd get nothing.

But in the glove compartment of his car, encased in clear plastic, was the five of spades. That is nothing the police can use against him; even though playing cards were left at all the murder scenes, it is simply not illegal to possess one.

But Laurie, Pete, and I realize it is an ominous development. We now have a good idea why Z was staying in this area.

He must have a target.

The next steps are all too predictable. Z's attorney has already shown up. He is with a Fort Lee office and does not come cheap. There will be an arraignment tomorrow, and the judge will no doubt grant bail.

The three charges against Z are not insignificant, but not enough to keep him held over. Bail might be hefty, but I have no doubt that after the hearing tomorrow, Z will make bail and be freed.

Sam Willis's report on Z's phone yields nothing helpful. He's made seven calls in the last week. Four were to local restaurants, apparently to get food delivered to the hotel.

Two were to Apple customer service, and another was to a software company. Apparently he's been hungry and was having computer problems; neither of those are the kind of problems I was hoping we would cause him.

I call a meeting of the whole team, including Sam and Willie. We need to plan what our next steps are going to be.

Once we're gathered, I say, "Z is going to be released tomorrow, unless we get lucky and someone kills him in the jail. Assuming that doesn't happen, we need to tail him as best we can. The fact that there was a playing card in his car could easily mean he has another target in mind."

"It's possible that getting picked up could scare him off, but we certainly can't count on that. Some of these targets seem to have been chosen at random, so maybe he will just decide to move on to an easier job," Laurie says.

I don't respond, and Laurie says, "Corey?"

"Sorry. Something about what you just said reminds me of something, but I can't place it. If Z moves on, then there's nothing we can do. We don't have the capability of chasing him across the country. At least he'd be skipping bail, so the cops could send out a warrant for his immediate arrest.

"I don't know how much that would inhibit him, but it's something."

As meetings go, this one is depressing. We are all convinced this guy is a mass murderer, and we are hoping to someday get him on relatively minor charges. And we are pessimistic about even that.

But as long as he is in this area, keeping close tabs on him is crucial. It would be awful to wake up one morning and hear about another "playing-card" murder.

Sam Willis promises to keep tabs on Z's phone calls, as well as the GPS device in it. If we lose him, we hope we can learn his location that way, although last time he was smart enough to ditch his phone.

We still don't know what has been behind all these murders: we have not been able to logically understand their pattern. But now that matters far less than preventing the next one.

If we had the man- and womanpower to do so, I would like to keep an eye on Emile Mateo. He has taken over Espinosa's operation, which makes him a suspect in Espinosa's killing.

We know he didn't pull the trigger himself; we believe that was Z, since Sam is positive that Z was in the area at the time of the shooting. Mateo might have paid Z to do it, and Z might now be working for him.

Maybe Mateo has other people he wants to get rid of, possibly one or more of Espinosa's men who Mateo cannot trust. That could be why Z has chosen to stay in the area, despite the legal jeopardy he is obviously in.

All we can do is wait and see.

The arraignment goes as expected. Z doesn't say a word other than "Not guilty," and his lawyer successfully argues for bail. The prosecutor takes the opposite position, but does so knowing he has little chance to prevail. The police just do not have enough on Z to keep him in jail until trial.

I would be shocked if a trial ever takes place.

Z walks out of the courtroom, a smile on his face, staring at me. Right now Russo's suggestion that we have Marcus kill him is sounding better and better.

THREE DAYS OF WATCHING Z'S HOTEL HAS GOTTEN US ABSOLUTELY nowhere.

As far as we can tell, he has not gone anywhere at all; he certainly hasn't used his car. We haven't been watching him 24-7. We've left at ten each night and picked it back up at seven in the morning.

I doubt that he's gone anywhere during that time. According to Sam the phone hasn't moved, and if Z's been out with the car, he's been smart enough to park it in the exact same space, at the same slight angle, when he's returned.

There is always the chance that he has gone out a side door and had someone pick him up. He might not even be in the hotel at all anymore, although according to Sam he hasn't checked out. And again, if he left, he did so without his phone.

I think he's still there, and I think he is playing with us.

I take over on the fourth day, arriving at seven o'clock in

the morning. This is my second time on this shift, which means I have to get up at five thirty. Dani thinks I'm a dairy farmer.

I alternate between sports talk radio, music, and news programming, none of which are enough to prevent me from going crazy. Simon is with me; I think he prefers music because he basically sleeps during the other two.

The funny thing is that in all my years on the force, I was never on a stakeout, not once. But even though it's normally a cop's job, here I am doing it after my retirement. If I were Simon, I'd be pissed off about it.

At twelve fifteen, I see Z come out of the hotel; it's such a surprise I do a double take to make sure. If he knows I'm here, he doesn't betray it. He looks around some, but not in my direction.

He might know there's a possibility he's being watched, if not by us then by the police. But he seems unconcerned. I've got a feeling we are heading for the diner.

Z gets in his car and pulls out of the parking lot. I fall in behind him, keeping my distance. I'm better at following people than I am at stakeouts; I certainly enjoy it more.

He does not go on either the Turnpike or the Garden State Parkway. Instead he goes onto city streets and we wind up on a street that is two lanes in each direction, with a speed limit of forty-five. Few cars are on the road; we're in an upscale, residential neighborhood.

I drop a little farther behind, so as to make sure he doesn't see me. In a worst-case scenario, if I lose him, Sam can likely tell me where he is by the phone GPS.

It's possible he's spotted me, though, because he starts to speed up. I increase my speed as well, and before I know it, we're both going seventy. We are entering a dangerous area, and I am not going to go faster no matter what he does.

And he increases his speed . . . steadily . . . dramatically.

We're on a straightaway, so I can see him, but he's getting smaller and smaller in the distance. He must be going ninety, maybe a hundred. There is no way he can safely drive at this speed.

He's gone; I simply cannot see him anymore. I slow down to fifty; if I can't keep up with him anyway, then there's no sense in my driving dangerously. I'll keep going in this direction and see what happens.

I call Sam Willis, who answers on the first ring. "Sam, I need you to follow the location of Z's phone GPS."

"Okay. You want me to do it while you hold on?"

"Yes, please. He has been traveling west on . . . never mind, Sam. I'll call you back."

Up ahead, along the side of the road, is a fireball that used to be a car. As I get closer, I can't tell if it is Z's car, but I'd bet anything that it is. The car hit a telephone pole, knocking it over, but based on the result, I would still say that the pole emerged the winner in this confrontation.

I park and run toward the burning car, but I have to back off because of the intense heat. It doesn't matter; if Z is in that car, which he must be, there is no saving him.

He's not playing with us anymore.

IF YOU TOLD ME I COULD LIST THREE HUNDRED THINGS THAT Z MIGHT DO, suicide would not have been on the list.

And then if you asked me to list a hundred possible ways he might kill himself, speeding and driving a car into a pole would never have entered my mind. I would have thought he would get access to a gun and blow his brains out.

Shows what I know.

I can't enter the mind of a person like Z, which I suppose is something I should be pleased about. But he certainly didn't seem the type to be stricken by a guilty conscience, and he definitely seemed confident enough to believe he could escape from any danger.

That he was facing three relatively minor charges should simply not have been enough to make him end it all.

Yet he did.

I saw him get into the car with my own eyes; it was not a

body double. The body was burned well beyond recognition, but I have no doubt that the police will test the DNA and determine that it was in fact Z who died in that blaze.

I'm certainly not sorry that he's dead; the world will be a better place for it. But I sure wish I knew why he did it.

It defies logic.

I head home; there is nothing more to accomplish here. I head for Laurie's house, after calling her and telling her we need a meeting of the team.

"We solved the case we were given," I say to Marcus and Laurie once we're all here. We usually do a postmortem to analyze a case when we're finished with it.

In this case, *postmortem* is an apt term, since everybody involved is dead. Vogel, Baskin, Espinosa, and Z . . . they're all gone. Officially the initial case might never be closed, but justice has been served, and that will have to be good enough.

"I agree," Laurie says. "There are still plenty of questions that I'd like answered, but we did what Pete asked us to do. It doesn't feel fully satisfying, but I think it's time to move on to the next one."

"What do we do about the murders in those other cities?" I ask.

"Not much we can do except tell the local detectives everything we learned. They'll be in the same place we are on our case; they'll know who did it, but the perpetrators are already dead. My guess is that they'll notify the families and move on."

"They won't know the why," I say. "And neither do we."

"Actually, ours is the only case in which we do have a good idea of the why. Vogel was informing on Espinosa to the Feds, so Espinosa had him killed. Baskin was wrong place, wrong time."

"I wish I could be as sure as you."

She smiles. "I'm not sure at all."

ANDY AGREES WITH ME THAT IT'S FINALLY OKAY TO END BILL SAMPSON'S protection of Dani.

We were worried about her because of the photographs that Z had taken, but Z is obviously no longer a threat. DNA has identified his charred remains, which I knew would happen.

His death is listed as a suicide, and that is probably accurate. There was no reason for him to drive at such insane speed on that street. He wasn't being chased, nor was he chasing anyone. I know that . . . I was there.

Sam is the only one who offers a possible different explanation. He says that a hacker might have taken over the computer system in the car and removed it from the control of the driver. Said hacker could have increased the speed to peak levels, until the car hit the tree. The hacker could even have locked the doors; in that scenario Z would only have been able to watch in horror.

I wouldn't dream of challenging Sam's claim that it could happen; I am constantly amazed at the technical things that people can come up with. I just don't think it happened here.

The obligatory police examination of the car comes up empty. They were looking more for a defect in the car that caused it to speed up on its own, but the car was simply too totally destroyed to yield any such information.

Laurie, Marcus, and I plan to meet in a couple of weeks to discuss the next cold case we are going to take. Three others were on Pete's list, so maybe it will be one of those, or maybe we'll ask him to give us more alternatives. He showed a willingness to do that.

Pete has made no secret of his pleasure with the way we handled the Vogel/Baskin murders. He is going to declare the case solved, officially blaming Z for the murder and Espinosa for ordering it. That is probably right, it's certainly close enough, and no one is going to come along and challenge it.

Pete tells us that Emile Mateo has in fact taken over Espinosa's operation, and Mateo has done so with authority. At least two of his rivals have been eliminated in a way that suggests Mateo is a worthy successor to Espinosa in ruthlessness.

My suggestion to Joseph Russo that we could bring down the entire Espinosa drug operation, which I knew was nonsense when I made it, has been exposed as an empty promise. Russo will have to contend with the same level of competition that he did before.

Oops.

I haven't heard from him about it, but my guess is that we will not have any more idyllic meetings on the grass of Eastside Park.

Dani, Simon, and I are taking advantage of the end of the

case, plus a happy coincidence involving her work, to go on an extended vacation. She's handling an event in Asbury Park. It won't be time-consuming, other than on the day of the event, so we're going to spend a couple of weeks down there.

She's gone ahead to rent a house and deal with some work stuff, and I'm going to meet her down there tomorrow. We both like the shore, especially at this time of year, before the end of the school year when it's not so crowded.

She's called to tell me that she's gotten a nice place on Kingsley Street, near the ocean. She forgot the street address, but will email it to me. I'm looking forward to it, especially because I know how much Simon loves going in the ocean.

We learned of his love for it just about a year ago, and now when we're down there, we take him to the beach early in the morning, before the humans arrive and get in the way. He loves when we throw a tennis ball in the surf and he can jump in and retrieve it.

I have only one more task to do on the case, and while I'm not looking forward to it, it has to be done. Brenda Crews, Vogel's mother, had asked me to tell her if I learned who killed her son, and I promised I would do so.

Having said that, I'm not going to be straight with her. I'm not going to tell her that Chris was likely a conspirator to mass murder, nor that he was using and selling drugs. It's dishonest of me, but I understand and accept that.

There is simply no upside to her knowing these things, and I'm not going to be the one to tell her.

So once again I am heading down to Freehold to the Castle Village apartments. I've called ahead to tell her I'm coming with more news. She doesn't ask me what it is; it's possible she no longer cares that much. She knows beyond any doubt that her son is dead; that faint hope that she held on to for years is gone. The rest of it is just not that important.

Miss Crews buzzes me up as before and is once again waiting for me at the door. She looks older and frailer than even the last time I saw her; these years and events have taken a tremendous toll on her, and that decline has accelerated since the K Team has gotten involved.

I feel bad about that, but I don't see how we could have handled it differently. On the plus side, we did give her certainty and closure, for whatever that is worth.

Once we're settled and she's served me coffee and more of those fantastic cookies, I say, "I promised I would tell you what happened to Chris, and who was responsible."

"I appreciate that."

"A drug dealer named Espinosa hired a professional killer to do it. Both Espinosa and the killer are now dead as well."

"Why did they want to hurt Chris?"

I've thought about how I would answer this question, and this is the best I could come up with. "Chris was helping the police against them, he was doing good, and they found out about it."

She could ask me why Chris was in a position to take down a drug dealer, but much to my relief she doesn't. Instead she asks, "What about the poor Baskin girl?"

"She had nothing to do with it. She had the bad luck to be in the wrong place at the wrong time."

We talk a little more, and she finally asks, "Did you ever learn whether Chris knew those people in those cities?"

"What are you talking about?"

"The people you asked me about last time you were here."

I am almost too stunned to respond, but I finally manage, "No, we never learned that."

She shakes her head sadly. "None of this makes sense."

I have one more question for her, and when she answers it, suddenly what made no sense makes total sense now.

And suddenly I'm in no mood to go on vacation. Brenda Crews has just given me a gift that is a hell of a lot better than a B-minus in freshman English.

I SPEND ABOUT FIVE HOURS TRYING TO MAKE SURE I'M RIGHT.

I look at it from every angle I can think of, and even though I do not understand it, I know it to be real. It's not logical, which may be the point.

My first stop in my effort to prove my theory is Professor Sharperson. I need to delve into his predictive theory in more detail; it can tell me a lot about this case . . . maybe all I need to know.

It being Saturday, he's not teaching classes today, but when I called him, he once again invited me to his Matawan home. He said he will be out most of the day, so asked if I could come at 7:00 P.M.

It's the fourth time I'll be seeing him, and he said he was impressed by my diligence. Having a professor impressed with me about anything is a first. My previous best experience with a teacher was when Brenda Crews gave me that B-minus.

Matawan is about an hour from Paterson, but Simon and I hit bad traffic on the Garden State Parkway. It's going to make me about a half hour late, but when I call Sharperson to tell him and apologize, he says it's no problem, that he has no plans for the evening.

When I arrive, he once again gets me a Diet Coke and spends some time marveling about what a beautiful dog Simon is. "I assume he's house-trained?"

"Perfectly. He's probably insulted that you brought it up."

He laughs. "Sorry about that." Then, "I hope you've already had your dinner. All I have is three slices of two-day-old frozen pizza."

"Sounds delicious, but I'm fine."

"I'm actually very glad you came down. I was going to call you anyway."

"Why is that?"

"I saw on the news that your friend Mr. Espinosa was killed. After our last meeting, you can imagine that it piqued my interest."

Sharperson had read Espinosa's psychological profile the last time we met, as I was asking him how Espinosa might react. He correctly predicted that Espinosa would send his people at me, but come himself the second time if the first try was unsuccessful.

"You were right about his approach," I say. "He was coming at me himself the second time, but someone intervened."

"Who was that?"

"The person I want to talk to you about. His name is, or at least the name he went by, is Z."

"Z? That's all?"

I nod and start to describe everything I know about Z, up to and including my belief that he killed Espinosa.

"You seem to attract dangerous people," he says when I'm finished.

"Tell me about it."

"So how can I help you regarding this Z? You referred to him in the past tense; I assume he is no longer among the living?"

"Correct." I describe Z's death, recounting the high-speed suicidal trip into the telephone pole.

"Extraordinary."

"Based on your predictive theory, does it surprise you that a guy like that would commit suicide?"

"That's a very difficult question because I am only hearing your description of him and his life. There is obviously a huge amount that you, and therefore I, don't know. Based on what you have related, suicide seems unlikely. But I say that with so many caveats as to render my comment fairly meaningless. I'm sorry."

I nod. "Understood. Let me add some hypotheticals."

"Suppose he also committed a series of murders around the country, leaving playing cards in each case, as he did with Vogel and Baskin."

"That wouldn't impact my view as to his potential for suicide."

"Fair enough. Suppose he was working for a single entity in all of those cases."

"Not following."

"Suppose one of the people he was working for was an asshole college professor . . . let's say, at a school like Rutgers."

Simon growls; he has seen the gun that has appeared in Sharperson's hand before I did. Sharperson is much quicker than I expected.

He has a smile on his face, with the gun pointed at my face. That is not where I want it pointed.

"Take it easy, Simon," I say. "Down."

Simon goes down, but he's not happy about it. He wants to go after Sharperson; Simon does not have a fearful bone in his canine body.

"I'm impressed," Sharperson says. "You are smarter than you appear. Though obviously not smart enough to avoid your current predicament."

"I'm also not smart enough to know why you did it."

He actually chuckles. "That's the entire point, so don't be so hard on yourself. No one is smart enough to know why we did it, because there is no reason. Do you understand? No reason. None of it could be predicted, and none of it could be understood, because it was entirely random."

"I'm not following," I say, even though I am.

"Then let me put it in words you can understand," he says condescendingly. "You drove here today. There are literally millions of routes you could have taken. You could have turned down any series of streets; you could have come here by way of Iowa if you wanted to."

"So?"

"So let's say I wanted to intercept you on your route. I would have gone to Google Maps, found the fastest and shortest route and assumed you would take it. Then I could have intercepted you, because you would have been acting predictably. But if you had let the choice of your route be made totally at random, I could not have done so."

"So the cards made the choice of who would be killed."

"Exactly. So how could you or anyone predict it, or solve it?"

"Yet here I am."

He frowns slightly. "Yes, because my colleague chose to leave the playing cards. It was a conceit; he considered it harmless, but it was not. Never mind, the wonderful thing about this work is that it is ongoing. Until my death, when it will all be published."

"You've kept a record?" I'm recording this to my phone; if I get out of this alive, Sharperson is history.

"Certainly. I'm an academic. This has been an academic exercise. But I must say an invigorating one. My colleagues were far more interested in that side of it."

"You can teach a prison class."

He laughs. "You do have nerve, I'll tell you that. I hope you're recording everything. I can submit it as an appendix to my paper."

"I'm actually wearing a wire, so the police are hearing it. They should be coming in any moment."

A quick flash of worry is replaced by a return of confidence. "I think not. You're too predictable; you made the mistake of thinking you could handle this entirely on your own."

"I can," I say, although the gun pointed at my face presents a different point of view.

Simon is still poised, waiting for my command, but Sharperson is maybe eight feet away. Simon couldn't make it in time from his current position.

"I think not. At this point your life expectancy can be measured in seconds."

"Your neighbors will hear the shot."

"Perhaps. But kids in the neighborhood set off firecrackers all the time. No one in hearing distance will recognize the difference. You have no idea what a bad night this is for you, Mr. Douglas. Too bad you won't be around to see all of it."

I have no idea what he is talking about, but it's clear that he is referring to something else that is going to happen tonight. He believes I will be dead and not here to see it. It's an ominous thing for him to say, and it worries me. "What do you mean?"

He doesn't answer the question. All he says is, "Time to go, Mr. Douglas."

"Gun," I yell, and Simon springs into action, heading for

Sharperson. Simon has no chance to make it, and Sharperson, taken by surprise, starts to move the gun.

I stand up quickly, drawing my own gun. Sharperson looks back at me, as I knew he would, but doesn't adjust the level at which he was firing. So instead of hitting me in the face, he hits me in the chest.

I'm jolted back by the force of the bullet, but protected by my bulletproof vest. I don't think that Sharperson is wearing a vest himself, but since I like to be sure, I put my bullet into the center of his forehead.

He falls back as Simon reaches him, so I yell, "Off," and Simon quickly backs off. I consider it beneath his dignity to have him chewing on a dead guy.

I look down on him. "Let me put this in words you can understand. You are one dead academic."

I HOPE SHARPERSON WAS RIGHT ABOUT THE NEIGHBORS THINKING THE shots were fireworks.

I should be calling the local police right now, but I don't want to do that. I want to learn everything I can about what has been happening, and Sharperson told me he committed it to writing.

I hope it's not on his computer because I obviously wouldn't know his password, although if I had to guess, I'd go for *random*.

I don't see anything in the room I'm in, which is the den, so I start looking for his office. There cannot be a college professor on the planet that doesn't have an office. I find it; it's upstairs at the end of the hall. It's small, filled with books and a large desk strewn with papers.

He is a sloppy dead academic.

Also on the desk is his computer. I open it and it springs to life, but immediately demands a password. I type in *random* three ways, all lower case, all caps, and a cap *R*. None of them work, so I move on.

The desk drawers are not locked, so I quickly go through them but find nothing that interests me. I look in the closet and see a square metal box that looks like a filing cabinet. I go to open it and it's locked, which substantially increases my interest in it.

I look out the window to see if there is any unusual activity in the neighborhood. Obviously I want to see if police have been called to the scene, but I also want to know if curious neighbors are milling about.

There's nothing, the street is dark and silent. It's Saturday night, so maybe people are out at parties . . . it's high school reunion season. Or maybe they haven't heard the shots or think it's those damn kids and their fireworks.

Well, those kids are about to strike again.

I fire at the lock on the box, doing so at an angle so as not to damage anything inside. It opens; filing cabinet locks are generally not built to withstand gunfire.

The inside of the box has plastic sheets around all the sides and bottom. It was obviously done to protect the papers in the box, perhaps from moisture. This has to be what I'm looking for.

It is.

I take out what looks like a journal; the pages are hand-printed in ink. He may have been a slob when it came to his desk, but he was a neat freak when it came to this journal.

I open the first page and it says, "Predictive Theory: A Study of Random Action and Its Potential to Influence All Aspects of Human Life."

I start to skim through it quickly, and each page is more stunning than the one before it. It's written in a way I imagine one would write a research paper, or a dissertation, though I can't say that I've read any of those.

But it chronicles every single thing that has happened throughout the conspiracy, as well as the way decisions were made. They were not made by humans; they were made by playing cards.

Under the journal is the most amazing thing of all. The cards are there, and each one has the name of a victim on it, or an action that was taken. Sure enough, the king of clubs has Chris Vogel's name on it. There is even a card that says, "Reveal the location of the bodies."

There are more than the six victims we know about. Obviously murders were committed in which the detective did not input the playing card clue into the NCIC system. Either that or playing cards in those cases were not left with the bodies.

The last card is the most chilling of all.

It is the five of spades.

That's the same card that was found in the glove compartment of Z's car when he was brought in for questioning. At the time we made the natural assumption that it was meant to be left near the body of the next victim.

The name of that projected victim is, like the others, at the top of the card.

Dani Kendall.

I USED TO TAKE PRIDE IN THE FACT THAT I NEVER PANIC. THAT CLAIM IS NOW
officially out the window.

I have never in my life been this scared; there is a pit in my stomach the size of Peru.

I now know what Sharperson meant when he said that I wasn't going to be around to fully see what a bad night this would be for me. Someone is going to make an attempt on Dani's life . . . if they haven't already.

I race to my car, Simon along with me, not even bothering to close the door to the house behind me. If anyone walks in, they are going to find an academic with a bullet in his head. I don't care.

I have got to get to the house in Asbury Park.

Then I am hit by another wave of fear when I realize that I don't know which goddamn house it is. Dani never sent me the actual address.

It should take me a half hour to get to Asbury Park, but I'm going to make it much faster. I just need to know where the hell within the city the house is.

I call Dani and there is no answer, freaking me out even more. Next I call Sam Willis, who answers as always on the first ring.

"Sam, I need help immediately. It is life-and-death." I give him Dani's cell phone number. "I have to know the address where that phone is. And I need to know within fifteen minutes."

"I'm on it," he says, not taking the time to ask any questions. "I'll call you back."

I should call Pete next, or the Matawan police, and tell them what is waiting for them at Sharperson's house. But I almost can't form the words, and on some level I don't want anything to take away from my focus on Dani, even though I can do nothing except drive and wait for Sam to call.

I try Dani a couple more times, but still no answer. I don't want to keep calling because I don't want Sam to get a busy signal when he calls me back.

Finally, when I'm about five minutes from Asbury and going at high speed, Sam calls. I just say, "Sam."

"Three eighty-four Kingsley Street."

That's the street Dani told me she took the house on, so I am encouraged that he's right.

I don't even thank him; there will be time for that later. Right now I just want to focus on driving and getting to 384 Kingsley Street.

I am petrified about what I am going to find there.

I don't know exactly where 384 is, but fortunately Dani had told me we were in walking distance of the boardwalk. So that's where I start, working my way inland.

I drive two and a half blocks until I see 379 on the left side of the street. I park there, and Simon and I jump out so we can approach 384 on foot and paws. I take my phone with me.

The house is dark except for some lights toward the back. I hope Sam has the right house; I remember he has in the past said that this kind of GPS information is not exact. It could conceivably be a house on either side. But for now I have to assume and hope this is the right one.

I press redial on the phone and hear Dani's phone ringing toward the back of the house. That the phone is back there but she is not answering is absolutely horrifying, but I can't let my mind go there.

I have to do what I can do. I have to control what I can control.

Simon and I race up the narrow cement driveway toward the back of the house; I have my gun out and I'm holding it in my right hand. It's dark back there; there's little moonlight and all I can see by is the reflected glow from the lights in the house.

"Don't take another step, Douglas."

In the dim light I can see Dani. Harold Collison is standing behind her, holding her in front of me with his arm around her neck. "There's a gun in your girlfriend's back, so take your gun out nice and slow and throw it behind you."

All Dani says is "Corey."

Even though I'm just fifteen feet from him, I don't think he can see my gun. He wouldn't have told me to take it out if he could. They are farther toward the back of the house, where the light is. Where Simon and I are, it's that much darker.

Simon is to my right, almost against the house. I don't know whether Collison even knows he is there.

"I don't have a gun," I say, slowly walking toward him. Simon walks closer as well, following my lead.

"Then in ten seconds you won't have a girlfriend. Throw the gun now."

"Okay, okay." I reach into my pocket and take out my phone.

I toss that behind me; it makes a significant noise in the otherwise total quiet of the driveway.

"Now walk slowly toward me; we're all going for a ride."

I walk toward him, which is what I wanted to do all along. I still don't think he sees Simon, and I am concealing the gun as best I can.

We've got to be less than ten feet away when Simon steps on something . . . maybe a branch, maybe some leaves. There's a slight rustling noise, and I hear Collison say, "What the . . ."

"Gun!" I yell, and Simon heads for him at a full run, going from zero to sixty faster than a Ferrari. At that same moment, Dani makes a sudden move to get away from him.

Collison is confused and hesitates, scared at whatever is snarling at him in the darkness. A split second later, that hesitation costs him, as Simon is on his gun arm, ripping it apart and causing the gun to fall to the pavement.

Collison screams in pain, as perfect a sound as any I can remember hearing.

"Off!" I yell, and Simon lets him go. I'm not quite so nice about it. I punch him in the face, and then again, and then again. He moans, so I hit him again, and he crumples to the ground.

For a moment I think he is unconscious, but then he moves. I would take extreme pleasure in shooting him, and for the moment I consider it, but then I think better of it and kick him in the side of the head.

He doesn't move anymore.

I go to Dani and wrap my arms around her.

"I can't believe you got here." Then, "I have never been so scared."

"Join the club. Join the club."

I HEAD BACK FOR THE PHONE THAT IS LYING ON THE GROUND, THE ONE THAT Collison thought was a gun.

I call Pete Stanton on his cell phone, and I try to stop my hands from shaking so that I can hold the phone to my ear. I relate as best I can what happened and give him the address that we're at, and Sharperson's address in Matawan.

"So Sharperson is dead and Collison is alive?"

"Yes and probably yes. I beat the shit out of him. I need to call the Asbury Park cops."

"Let me do it. I know a guy there. Then I'll call the Matawan cops and go out there with some of our people. It's our case because of Vogel and Baskin."

"Pete, there's a file cabinet in his office. I shot the lock off and looked through it. You've got to keep custody of it; the answers to everything are in there."

"I'm on it."

"Thanks, Pete. And if you get a chance, can you call Laurie and update her?"

"What am I, your admin?"

"I think of you more as an intern. I'll wait here for the Asbury cops."

"You do that."

I get off the phone and hug Dani again; I think I am going to be doing this a lot, although right now I'm using one hand and holding a gun on Collison with the other. He hasn't moved, but I'm not taking chances.

Neither is Simon; he's watching Collison intently. Simon is still one hell of a cop.

"I am so sorry I put you through this," I say to Dani, who seems remarkably calm, given her evening. It's the first of probably five thousand times that I will say it.

"And I am so glad you got here. And I'm really glad you brought Simon, the single greatest dog in the world."

The Asbury Park police are slower to arrive than I would have expected, though I can't be sure that Pete called them right away. They're still here within ten minutes, and they come in force.

I tell them I'm armed and they tell me to put the gun on the ground. They can't be quite sure who is a good guy and who is a bad guy and do not want to take any chances until they have a full understanding as to what is going on. It's the proper police procedure.

A plainclothes cop approaches me. "Corey Douglas?"

"That's me."

"I'm Lieutenant Duffy. Pete Stanton called me."

"Glad to meet you, Lieutenant. This is Dani Kendall."

He nods. "Are you both okay?"

"We are." I point to Collison, who is moving ever so slightly. "He's not."

"We'll deal with him."

Lieutenant Duffy tells us we can wait in the house and sends two officers in with us. We're in there for two hours while the cops take control of the scene and forensics people do their work. Then they separate Dani and me and we give our individual statements. Simon stays with me, but does not give a statement.

We're told we can go outside, and waiting for us are Laurie, Marcus, and Pete. Laurie said that Andy had to stay home with Ricky; they couldn't get a babysitter at this hour.

Pete says that the filing cabinet is secure and in the possession of the Paterson cops, which I am glad to hear.

"Are there any other people you killed or beat up tonight?" Pete asks. "Maybe it skipped your mind?"

I pretend to think about it and remember. "No, I think that's it. But the night is young."

After we all talk for a while, I ask Dani where she wants to spend the rest of the night.

"Home. Please . . . let's go home."

HAROLD COLLISON WILL NEVER SEE THE LIGHT OF DAY AGAIN.

Obviously he has the financial wherewithal to hire the best lawyers, but they haven't invented the lawyer that can get him off the hook. That's because his partner Professor Bruce Sharperson meticulously detailed every aspect of the conspiracy.

Sharperson provided a road map that any prosecutor could follow, and it amounts to a confession on Collison's behalf.

Ironically, Sharperson disdained his colleagues. While he saw himself as creating an academic exercise to advance his demented theories, Collison and Vogel were in it for different reasons.

Both of them were essentially thrill seekers. The idea of turning themselves over to the random whim of the cards, with no option to disobey, was invigorating in a way they'd never before experienced and could not get enough of.

It was almost a religious experience for them; they put their trust in something outside themselves. Sharperson mocked their attitude in his writings, but used them to further his goals.

Sharperson's thesis was to demonstrate that the only things that humans could not understand or defend against were random acts. All people naturally, instinctually tried to predict what was to come, and to effectively deal with it, based on logic.

But randomness has nothing whatsoever to do with logic. The murders around the country, as well as that of Kim Baskin, were dictated by the cards. There was no rational reason for them to have been chosen as victims. How could their murders be solved if there was no reason for them to have been committed in the first place?

Vogel was essentially an employee of the conspiracy. He traveled to the cities and cased out the victims. For that, Collison wired money to him.

Ironically, the decision to kill Vogel was made because he revealed to his partners that he was talking to the Feds about Espinosa. That correctly made him unreliable in their eyes; if he could inform on Espinosa, then he might someday inform on them.

Vogel's murder was the first act not dictated by the cards, and Sharperson acknowledged as much in his journal. Once we were on the case, then he and Collison made a series of measures to counter us. None were random; all were predictable . . . and they led to the conspirators' downfall.

However, the last act was in fact to be random. All of our names were on playing cards, and they picked Dani's.

It was Collison's idea to leave playing cards at the scenes, and Sharperson was not happy about it. Once again, it spoke to predictability, the exact thing he was trying to avoid.

If I wanted to, I could go on a national tour . . . sort of like Springsteen without the talent. Each of the cities where a murder was committed—there were eight—wants to wrap up its case. The local cops want me to explain the details of the conspiracy to them, so they can do so.

Traveling like that is the last thing I want to do, so I suggest Zoom sessions. I even get Dani to teach me how to do it, which is to click on the link they send me. It's difficult, but I've got it mastered.

So I'm spending my time doing these online tutorials, explaining to the local cops what happened. Sharperson chose a city by picking cards, then took names out of a phone book, and chose a victim the same way.

Then Vogel, at least for the murders that took place while he was alive, went to the town and reported to Z what the setup was, and what he needed to know. Z came to town, did the job, and left.

Z was a total professional, which is why Sharperson and Collison paid him a large amount of money to work for them. He left no clues behind, and the police certainly had no motives to follow up on. They had no way to know that the victims were randomly chosen.

Once I'm done with these Zoom calls, my K Team partners and I will meet to discuss the wrap-up of the case. Laurie has already told me she wants to know how I realized it was Sharperson and Collison.

I take Dani and Simon out to dinner. The media is painting me as something of a hero, but Simon has not been getting the credit he so richly deserves. Fortunately, Simon is humble and prefers biscuits to acclaim.

Dani has been uncharacteristically quiet in the two days since that night. I haven't tried to get inside her head; I can't imagine what it must be like for her. I'm used to these things, and the thought of her being in danger was close to paralyzing.

As the person in the actual danger, and as someone who hasn't lived this kind of life, it must be totally disorienting.

Once we're settled in, I ask, "Are you okay?"

"I think so. I keep replaying it over and over in my mind. I know I shouldn't, but I can't help it. If you were five minutes later—"

"I wasn't."

"I never told you the address. I realized that while he had me. How did you find me?"

"I'm a master detective. And Sam Willis is a genius; he traced the GPS on your phone."

"I'll call and thank him."

"You can make him eggs." Then, "So where are we?"

"What do you mean?"

"This is my world. I'm not saying you'll ever be in this situation again, but I probably will. Can you handle that?"

"Your job is not the only dangerous one. Last week I did an event, and three people got sick from eating bad pieces of sushi."

"I'm sorry you had to go through this. You can't imagine how sorry I am."

"Why? I didn't have any of the sushi."

"You know what I mean."

She nods. "I do, and I'll deal with it. When you're with someone, you have to take the good with the bad. And you bring plenty of good."

"SO HOW DID YOU KNOW?" LAURIE ASKS.

"It was the result of years of dedicated training; you have no idea how perfectly honed my detective skills are."

"Bullshit."

I nod. "That's another way of looking at it."

Laurie, Marcus, and I are in Laurie's den. Simon is with Laurie and Andy's three dogs; they're in the backyard playing. I think Andy is playing video games with Ricky in his room.

"So are you going to tell us?"

"I am, but it started with something small and then it built on itself. And to be completely honest, I still wasn't positive it was them until I was in Sharperson's house. I confronted him, and he pulled a gun on me. That seemed to indicate he wasn't your average college psych professor."

"What was the small thing?"

"Remember when Pete brought Z in for questioning on those

three lesser charges? Z seemed to be aware that we knew about Vogel going to those cities."

Laurie nods. "I remember that, but it wasn't definitive."

"Right. But I had asked Vogel's mother if she ever heard him mention the people that were murdered, without saying what happened to them. The next time I saw her, she mentioned that those people were from different cities, though I had never told her that.

"Collison was in touch with her. She must have mentioned it to him, and he must have asked if I mentioned the other cities. And he must have told Z that we knew about it, which is why Z said what he said under questioning."

"Not bad," Laurie says. "But that can't be all of it."

"Right, but that got me going. So once I thought it could be Collison and probably Sharperson, I put everything I knew through that prism, and it all seemed to fit."

"What do you mean?"

"Well, they certainly had the money to be paying Vogel, so that's where the wired money came from. Then there was the reunion list that Vogel told the head of the committee that he needed."

"What about it?"

"It was strange that he only kept the first page and circled a large chunk of the names. I counted the names he circled and there were fifty-two. I'll bet every one of those names was on a card and could have been the victim that night; Baskin just had the bad luck."

"Why did Z kill himself?" Laurie asks.

"I think Sam was right; I think the car was hacked. Collison is a computer genius; he could have done it. And remember Sam said that Z's phone showed a call to a computer company? It was Collison's software company."

"But why kill Z?"

"They were cleaning up loose ends. But the bottom line to all this, and what really got me thinking, was how random everything was. Ironically, it was so consistently random that it was predictable."

Marcus speaks for the first time. "When Z came to warn you in the park, he told you he was working for Espinosa. Why did he do that if he wasn't?"

"To throw us off. He had been following me; we know that from the pictures he took. He must have seen us go to talk to Alvarez at the DEA. They already knew that Vogel had been informing on Espinosa to the DEA, so Espinosa's name would have come up. This was their opportunity to get us to go after Espinosa.

"And that's why Z said he wouldn't give Espinosa the message to meet me in the park. He couldn't; he didn't work for Espinosa. He probably never said a word to him in his life."

Laurie nods her understanding. "And all those times that Sam reported the GPS data that showed Z was visiting Espinosa, he was wrong. He was there, but not to see Espinosa. It was rather to learn the layout so he would be able to kill him. Which he did."

"Exactly."

"So was Espinosa's death random?"

I shake my head. "I don't think so. I think things were getting out of control for Sharperson and Collison, and they killed Espinosa to get us to back off. Their hope was that we'd no longer have any reason to be involved if the person we thought killed Vogel and Baskin was dead."

"So they started behaving predictably," Laurie says.

"Right. And it did them in. Sharperson was right all along, but he didn't follow his own theory."

"And Russo was right," Marcus says. "I should have killed Z much earlier."

Andy comes in, a puzzled look on his face. "I thought I over-heard a conversation."

"That's because we're having a conversation," Laurie says.

"I mean between three people."

"We're three people," Laurie says.

Andy seems about to continue this, but shakes his head. "Never mind."

"While you're here, we're about ready for lunch," Laurie says. "Can you go pick it up?"

"Pizza would be good," I say.

"You guys are running up quite a tab."

I'M PAYING ONE FINAL VISIT TO BRENDA CREWS, BUT THIS IS A MUCH MORE enjoyable one.

Andy and I are bringing her Jasmine, an adorable seven-year-old beagle mix. Willie Miller has spoken to her and Mrs. Simmons, the neighbor who is going to share the dog with Miss Crews. He considers them an excellent home, and apparently Willie is a tough judge when it comes to homes for his rescue dogs.

It's love at first sight; Jasmine gets in Miss Crews's lap from the moment we arrive and shows no inclination to get off. Mrs. Simmons comes in and falls in love as well.

All is good.

Just before we leave, Miss Crews says, "I can't thank you enough, for everything. I wish I had given you a B-plus, or even an A."

"If I got an A in English, it would have triggered an investigation," I say. "There's one more thing we have for you."

"What's that?"

I hand her an envelope and tell her to open it after we leave.

"What is it?"

"Something else that Chris would have wanted you to have."

When she opens it, she'll find a check made out to her for $9,000.

We chose that amount because that's what we took from Espinosa's bagman Glover, which we kept.

We didn't pick the amount at random.